Lost in Montreal

Lost in Montreal

✳ Gay Walley

Incanto Press
Burlingame, California

Cover Illustration Copyright © 2014 by Incanto Press

Cover Art by Mike Medicine Horse, Assisted by Cynthia Medicine Horse and Melissa Sisk

Book Design and Production by Kate Davidson

Author Photograph by Steve Haag

Library of Congress Control Number: 2014939667

ISBN-13: 978-1-941217-00-9

Printed in the United States of America

1 2 3 4 5 6 7 8 9

This novel is dedicated to Gerrit Lansing
whom, when I said, "I'm a little blocked,"
responded with the advice, "Think of a place."
I wanted to write about Montreal.
I also dedicate this to both of my deceased parents,
who were the inspiration for these characters.

✳ One

I began a life of perpetual motion about the time of the Montreal streets. I was only fourteen and fifteen but I walked them with the intensity and cravenness of a mad woman. I walked them religiously, in the cold, in my yellow coat, with black boots, a yellowbird I called myself, in and out of cafes and bars. I sat in those heated bars with steaming coffees and cognacs while it snowed almost blindingly outside.

Fate was destined to find me. Find me in the French bistros I frequented each night and afternoon and some mornings. And while waiting, I sat at marble top tables—where the glass was set down in front of me with the quick ting of a jazz note and the colors of the cognac reflected the brown and gold of the St Lawrence—and I listened.

I listened to Hungarian sculptors who escaped their revolution, to French Canadian revolutionaries planning to frighten the English out of Quebec, to French Canadian conservatives comparing prices of Mustangs, to Polish men who left their country to escape poverty and were now being underpaid to paint apartments, to Czech film makers soon to go to Hollywood, to British men looking to sleep with French girls, any French girls, to Americans who were flummoxed at French menus and who laughed too loudly in their nervousness.

As one of the regulars in those bistros, I was nodded to, treated as one of the downtowners who came in and stomped her boots to get the snow off, shook the clingy whiteness off my coat, pulled off my painfully wet gloves, while anxiously looking around for a waiter to give an order to. I was one of the regulars, who smiled at everyone and was smiled back at, who cheered myself with the leering looks of the waiters and the men standing at the bar, or on the knowing smiles of the French dark eyed women in their tight short black skirts. I told myself I would learn from all of them a sexual fervor out of which I would fashion my own brand of allure.

I studied the men from my table—their furtive looks, the glances that kept returning to me. I learned which way to sit (crossed legs, angled), which smile (ironic, mischievous or secretive), which motion of the hand (quiet, like painting a watercolor). I learned what held them. And it wasn't as if I was an actress; my own screaming desire for love wanted to please those men. So I learned how to make a man feel more like a man, how suddenly he felt a little bigger standing next to you, if you smiled at him a certain way, how much he enjoyed becoming a little bigger. I learned these things for I knew they opened doors to learn even more.

At fifteen, I was on a marvelous journey of voices, hands, and eyes. Accented with cognac inside and blizzards outside.

Sometimes I tired of patrolling the bars by myself. Sometimes I stayed in a bistro a little longer. If the weather was too inclement or I was just too tired.

Sometimes, perhaps after many cognacs, I would sit up at the bar with the men, on a stool, and let one of them, the tallest usually, even then I was looking for power, let him pull my blue turtleneck up from my waist, and let him push my bra up toward my neck, his hairy hands gently circling my nipples, for both the man and I would be entranced at their abundant softness, and at the strangeness of this child face with woman eyes and woman breasts and a defiant large mouth that said, I can take it, I can, I really can, but would you, could you maybe help me.

I had parents. I had a father who raised me. I was finishing high school, a weekly boarder, who on weekends pretended I was visiting my mother, but instead would put eyeliner on and high suede boots if I had them and go down to the Mountain Street Bistro at around 11 a.m. on Saturdays and walk up and down the frozen streets till the insides of my cheeks were so cold that I had to go inside, Crescent Street to the Boiler Room or the Sir Winston Churchill Pub, down Mountain, up Guy.

Late at night I would go home with some man who would put a blanket over me and let me sleep chastely, drunkenly, and virginally on his couch.

I was too young, at fifteen, to want the responsibility of sex. I just wanted to be wanted. The men knew it too.

"So why don't you stay at your mother's?" my host would ask me the next morning.

"I don't live with her. She left when I was young."

"You know her?" he asked.

"Yes."

Silence.

"You know her too," I'd say.

"I do?" he'd ask.

"She's on TV. You know on *Face the Nation*. She does those bits—"

"The Viennese woman?"

"Yes," I said proudly, in spite of myself.

"Pretty."

"Yes."

He'd scrutinize me for similarities.

"So do you see her?" he'd ask, slightly bored.

I'd light a cigarette. While he was waiting for an answer, he'd turn toward his radio and put a French station on. There would be some American pop song being sung in French. The chirpiness made me cringe.

As he spoke, I would see my mother in many different frames of my mind. Mostly I'd see her as a frozen image. My mother and British father arriving from Europe on the Empress of France, me at one year old. My mother not married to my much older and broke father and already knowing she'd made a mistake, coming here with him, having a baby with him. He was fat, duller than she, pedantic, a man who holds a woman back. My mother stood at the ship's railing, taking in the cathedrals and fortressed buildings of Montreal as we steamed to the dock, and comforted herself in feeling sexually sated from having had an affair on the boat with the French Second Lieutenant Ferand. My father, on the other hand, was holding me. Both of us were looking at this small, clipped woman with a pretty Viennese face, who now turned to stare back at us coldly while wondering how quickly she could get away.

❋ Two

I remember my father having a garden party, during one of those dry, warm Canadian summer days. I had just learned to walk and I toddled and weaved in the sun from beer sip to beer sip and the adults seemed to enjoy it when I said, "More. More." The guests sat in those summer chairs, their legs extended, and I flirted with the men in rolled up white sleeves who so enthusiastically brought their glasses down to me. I loved all that smiling and all that climbing up onto knees and getting back down again and all that laughter and attention.

My father, delighted, said, "Look at her." He was big and flushed and, in his way, terribly alone amidst all these people. "She's getting drunk."

My mother dressed formally in those days, in elegant suits and expensive jewels, not at all appropriate to the suburban house we lived in in Ontario that had a plum and apple orchard adjacent to it. She looked like she was leaving for somewhere important every day.

She never smiled at me, unless we had guests and then it was an actress' smile. She seemed to smile easily with other people.

I was sure she hated me. She seemed angry at my existence. I just couldn't figure out why. I told myself, in some child language, that if I wanted to survive her, I must expect nothing from her. A toddler's attempt at Buddhism: I am not attached to my mother.

When I was four, my father and I took a walk in the fruit orchard, my white plastic boots crunching on the frosted earth. My father no doubt not dressed warmly enough, as if it were manly not to put on full gear, as if to weather the bad weather would make the Fates change their mind about him. Here was a real man, a victor, walking cavalierly through his apple and plum trees.

However, I could feel my father's sadness. Inside the house or having just left the house was that woman who was foreign, implacable, hard and lacking in tenderness for him. A woman who turned away from him and me. A woman who had worked for him in England and somehow thought he could take care of her. She had, unlike the rest of her family, survived the war. And he, he was of the victor race, the ones who saved the world from the Nazis. He just couldn't save what was left of their relationship.

And she, she didn't need him anymore. She was a woman who had that terrible lure for men. She was pretty, and, even moreenticing, she was needy.

So now she was humiliating him going off with the husbands round the neighborhood, disappearing for weeks and then returning when she was bored or the husbands missed their families.

At least that's how my father explained it to my four-year-old self.

My father took me with him when he went to console the betrayed wives, who were consoling him, perhaps in the same way the husbands were consoling my mother or my mother was consoling them.

He would say to me, "Well what can you do about it?"

My father using the word "nymphomaniac." "That is obviously what she is." We would drive back from our Florence Nightingale visits to these stunned wives and my father would talk to me about the shame of such a woman (my mother), unable to control herself, rushing about with all these men. I didn't understand about sex but understood you weren't supposed to go off with other people's husbands. She was an infidel, he said, self-serving, abandoning both him and myself, and apparently abandoning these well-behaved wives as well.

That cold Canadian afternoon in the orchard, I held onto his hand, my little gloves no doubt tied to my coat by the nanny. My father and I walked glumly around and I chattered away to try and make the whole problem of life seem worth it to him. I held his hand tighter, for his sake or mine I'm not sure.

"It's a bloody mess," he said looking up at the naked trees, in what seemed that long sad Canadian time between winter and spring.

We walked on and already the weak winter sun was turning in for the night.

We were both freezing but it was possibly warmer outside than in the house. At least here we could feel love for each other.

I mumbled something, while looking up at the almost giddy vastness of that immense star-dazzled night.

"Hmm?" he said. He put his hand on my face and said, "Don't worry. I know she's bloody awful but she'll be gone soon. She won't be able to stand it here."

I didn't really understand these words but if I did intuit she was leaving, I am sure I was not unhappy about it. We would be free. We could love each other in peace and quiet. I could love him and get on with my life, which would be to love my father.

Perhaps he felt the very same thing himself. He rubbed his eye and said, "It's getting cold, we'd better go in," and that is how my father and I began our life together.

✳ Three

I was just four when my father and I moved to Montreal. He rented an apartment on Decarie Boulevard, a commercial area of office buildings and 1950s apartment houses bordering a city highway. I remember the word Decarie. The way an Englishman said it, as opposed to how the French people who lived on the Boulevard said it. My father said it down tempo, enunciating every syllable, as if he was claiming it. De-Caah-Ree. The French said it fast and upbeat, like the word was in a car race. Dcree. It was as if there were two different streets.

My father heated corned beef hash out of tins for us to eat at night. Then he would go out for a drink at Ruby Foo's, the big Chinese restaurant that was the pride of Decarie Boulevard, and I would be frightened, alone in our furnished apartment. I was tense, from the fear of what would happen if he never came back. I had taught myself to put scotch in my milk to ease my tension. This, I believed, helped me forget the monsters hiding in doorways and on windowsills.

Eventually he would come home, and the unfathomable beings, at least the ones knocking against the windowpanes, would disappear.

Soon we took the upper half of a gray stone French Canadian duplex on St Mary's, I think it was called. It was from here I was to go to Grade One at Miss Edgars and Miss Cramps, a terrible name for a girls' school, if ever there was one.

After school, my father picked me up and sometimes walked with me in a nearby park. Parks must have reminded him of England. We walked through a park gracefully landscaped with those heavy, wide, Canadian maple trees that seem to augur a life of abundance. The park was maternal with those enveloping, leaning over branches, even if we did pass two cannons that commemorated ousting the British.

During those walks, he'd return to his favorite obsession: my mother. "Imagine her insane logic," he'd say, "telling me you'll be an adult longer than a child so it doesn't matter how she treats you now. Can you imagine?" he asked.

"No."

"Anyway," he continued, "there's no way on earth I would have let her have you. I told her, over my dead body you get Jacqueline."

"But I thought she doesn't want me," I replied.

"She doesn't. Of course not. But, even if she had, I wouldn't have let her. Not on a cold day in hell."

"But she doesn't want me," I repeated. There lay the aberration. Other mothers wanted their daughters.

But this did not seem to be so important to him. What he liked to repeat over and over was that he wouldn't have let her have me, even if she had wanted me.

Why was that?

I looked up at him, hoping he would clarify this, but he was drawing on his cigar, not seeing the women with scarves tied round their necks in elegant fur coats pushing baby carriages by us in the park.

Why did he go over this anyway? To give me my first lesson in male possessiveness? If you hurt a man, here's how he shows his upper hand? He takes away something you don't want anyway.

I'd look up at him, confused, but he'd smile happily down at me as if we had been planning a birthday party.

I would sigh and adjust the belt on my new school uniform. There were other difficulties to focus on anyway.

My father was turning out to be a somewhat unreliable roommate. He wasn't always nice to the nannies. I had liked my first nanny, Helena, the best. She was a big Austrian woman who seemed privy to my mother's affairs and both she and my mother constantly had to be told by my father that it was rude to speak German at the table. My father told me he got Helena drunk and that was how he found out about my mother's affairs. Affairs, he called them.

He laughed, however, when he heard me asking Helena if I would have "huge bozooms" like hers when I grew up. I don't know what she answered but she smiled worriedly at me, seeming to comprehend that this was not a fortunate home to be growing up in. However, after my mother left, Helena soon went to work for the Bronfmans in the Town of Mount Royale. This appealed to my father's British snobbishness. In other words, the Bronfmans who owned Seagrams had the same nanny as he who owned nothing.

The nannies that came after Helena all seemed to be Austrian too, like my mother, but not as tough. They had that unsteady tentativeness of the newly emigrated.

These nannies often started crying when my father came home, upset over breaking a dish or my not eating or something. What I couldn't understand was his response. My father, usually so indulgent with me, was stern and unreasonable with them.

"Maria," he'd say, as she cowered away from him after burning some casserole I didn't want to eat anyway, "have you gone mad? You can't go on working here if you can't manage a household. I've got too damn much to think about."

"Daddy, you don't have to make a big fuss of it," I'd pipe up, to defend the underdog. "I hate casseroles anyway."

"You don't know what you like or don't like."

"You said to always be polite," I'd say aggressively.

"Exactly."

"Well, then how come you're being rude?"

"Go to your room at once."

What I was to glean from this was that my father not only had unkind things to say about my mother, but this prejudice extended to other women too. Barmaids, however, were exempt and always "bloody nice women."

I decided that when I grew up, I better keep away from living rooms, kitchens and anything else to do with domesticity. There lay harbors of rage.

✳ Four

One afternoon I opened the unlocked apartment door after my day at Miss Edgars and Miss Cramps, only to be surprised by the strange vision of my mother sitting at the kitchen table. She wasn't supposed to be here.

To add to the confusion, my mother, that particular afternoon, was crying. She must have been thirty-one. She struck me as smaller than the larger-than-life icon that reigned in my imagination. She looked like a bent-over woman with a skullcap red haircut, red nails, a charm bracelet and red lipstick.

My father wasn't there.

Her chair was in the way of the refrigerator and I asked her—a test perhaps—if I could get some milk.

The next thing I knew I was flying down the stairs.

The fall was long, very very long, but the shove was sudden and in an instant I was crumpled up at the bottom landing, stung at the force of it.

Maybe I stayed there frightened because soon my father was picking me up, asking her what the hell had gone on. He put me in my bedroom and then they argued.

She never visited us again.

When she began living with a French journalist, I had turned five. My father and she had the upstanding idea I should have visits with her although none of us seemed to enjoy the reality of it.

When I was taken to see her, I would sit formally on one of her chairs, waiting to be taken somewhere or entertained in this strange apartment, but it seemed the planned entertainment was for me to watch her in her flowered dress kiss and giggle with her new husband,

Etienne. Between her nibbling at his moustache which was the height of disgustingness and their hands going all over the place which had them both laughing and then inexplicably silent, Etienne tried to tease me with boorish jokes like how he called opera pin cushion music because it sounded like someone sat on a pin. I appreciated that he tried.

However, as the interminable time passed, I was getting more and more nervous so I moved onto the arm of the armchair, not wanting to fully sit on the seat cushion, since that might mislead someone into thinking I was comfortable.

I slithered around on the leather arm of the chair watching them carefully, to see if I could get any clue to my mother's personality. That's when I fell on the floor. It was quiet, not a major fall but when I got back up, my arm hurt and seemed to have changed its shape, the elbow didn't seem to be where it was supposed to be, so I ventured over, embarrassed, to show them. I was frightened to draw attention to myself this way but, still, it was excruciatingly painful so, crying, I pointed out my arm to them, "Look, it's not right."

She leaned over and looked and didn't know what to do. Etienne came to assist with the examination; they moved me this way and that, and were confused at this oddity.

"What is going on?" they said. Then I was in an ambulance with her husband.

I had broken my arm.

My father came shortly to retrieve me from the hospital.

Maybe four years later, I was visiting her again, ice skating in the afternoon sun on the Mountain in Montreal. The skating area consisted of swirling ice paths traversing the mountain, which culminated in a big skating rink on top next to the Mountain Cafe. It was a freezing Canadian day, as always, but bright as cold days often are, and the adults were gently pulling the younger children along in trainer skates.

My mother, uncharacteristically, had come with Etienne to watch me. This was, I thought, because she had skated when she was in Vienna. Everyone skated in Vienna. That's what Vienna was. People playing musical instruments while ice skating or eating pastries on Liepzig horses.

"Where do you come up with these ideas?" my father had asked as I was enthusiastically explaining Viennese society to him.

"Everybody knows that," I said, exasperated with his British igno-
rance of the rest of the world.

"And when do you think she did this skating?"

"When she was my age."

He turned to the bar and took a pull at his cigar. His cheeks flushed out.

"It's possible, I suppose," he said, "but I think what really happened
was that she was in Czechoslovakia when she was your age. Living with
her grandmother. Maybe she skated there. It's possible," he said. "Hard
to imagine her making an effort at anything."

"I thought you said she's successful at her work." My mother was in
film and television. On the air and with a steady job. Compared to my
father, she seemed a beacon of stability.

"That's because she sleeps with everyone," he said.

I hated these oversimplifications of my father's. They were always
about the vagaries of being female and I was inevitably going to move
from being a child into a female, only a few more years to go, and there-
fore a little bit nervous about these outdated clichés he delivered with
such emphasis about my gender. Is this what happened to women? We
get written off in summary sentence structures?

"Alright," I said. "What do you think she did when she was my age?"

"I know what she did when she was a bit older," he said sarcastically.

"What?" I was fascinated about any facts about my mother. Could
anyone explain such a strange woman, not liking her daughter and all?
Who was she?

"What was she like at fourteen?" I asked, since this was an age I
aspired to. I was nine.

"At fourteen? Your mother had just arrived in Palestine."

"Palestine?"

"Her grandmother and uncles sent her there to get away from Hitler. They themselves went the other way, to Auschwitz."

I was appalled.

"When your mother got to Palestine, she located her motherwho
obviously didn't give much of a damn about her daughter either, having
gone to Palestine without her. A fine lot they were. Anyway, your mother set up life with her mother as a rich Jewess. And took piano lessons
because Mutti was a pianist."

My mind was reeling.

"Your mother has no ear for music," he added.

I looked askance at him. Was he making this up?

"But Mutti told me," he said, "that she caught Lisbeth having an affair with the piano teacher. At fourteen. That is your mother."

"So?" I said.

"She was a nymphomaniac even then."

His bitter tone of voice made me suspect this was not an even-handed diagnosis. Anyway I really was more interested in similarities between her and myself and, at nine, skating was more likely something we had in common so what the amorous piano teacher had to do with my original premise about the Viennese skating I did not know. My father could take a milkshake and turn it into an example of how my mother was profligate.

"You realize," he said, "you would have been gassed too, just for being related to her."

"Really?"

I was suddenly terrified, as if all this could happen now. More evidence that contact with my mother was more dangerous than I'd imagined.

But to go back to the day I was skating in the sun on the Mountain ice rink, I saw her in her white fur jacket and jaunty ski leggings, big sunglasses, and I began madly twirling on one skate, to prove that I was not the ineffectual dullard that she seemed to mistake me for. I twirled on one skate, and then began to skate backward at great speed. That's when I heard the Austrian raspy voice,

"Etienne," she said, "Look at her." At that precise moment, in the middle of my twirl, I slipped. I was down on the ice and the first thing that came to my mind was one more of my father's clichés: Pride comes before a fall.

Then I realized I couldn't move. Strange people were gathering around me. Other mothers, nice ones, were asking motherly questions. "Where does it hurt? Can you stand up?" I shook my head. My mother seemed confused and let the other mothers take charge.

Soon I was in an ambulance again. My leg was set in several places.

My father now had to carry me up the stairs to our apartment with my entire leg in plaster.

"It's rather expensive, these visits to your mother," he said, huffing and puffing.

For six months, he held my crutches and my arm as I hobbled in and out of his bars and he watched proprietarily as countless barmaids and barflies signed their name and well wishes to my leg. My mother and Etienne never added their own well wishes, but kept a cautionary eye as I crutched heavily around their apartment.

They could not wait, they said, until I grew up. Things would be, they said, much easier then.

✳ Five

Sunday nights were the social part of visiting her. That's when my father came to pick me up.

First he insisted on coming up to her apartment, not having me wait with the doorman.

I liked that my father came up to get me because I was a little proud of my mother's apartment as compared to my father's. My father's apartment had old scratched furniture, cigar ash all over the place, empty whiskey glasses, a black and white television on all the time.

My mother's apartment seemed to be all glass with its huge windows and I could see the lit cross at the top of the mountain at night and the French stone apartment houses with their circular iron stair railings and the glamorous lights of the city.

There were abstract paintings in my mother's apartment and the furniture, if not comfortable, was Swedish design with plush rugs and everything in her kitchen matched, even if she rarely used it, and everything was always clean and she often had flowers.

My father's place had the feel of a men's bar, with its old scratched furniture, cigar ash all over the place, empty whiskey glasses, a black and white television on all the time.

Every Sunday night I hoped my father got some hint, by standing in his big winter coat, which he wouldn't take off, in my mother's apartment, that this was the way sophisticated people lived.

He'd stand there waiting, not for me, but till my mother or Etienne, if he was there, offered him a drink.

Then he would say, "Very kind of you, indeed," and sat down.

Etienne would get him a drink.

My mother was silent, her lighter snapping quickly as she lit her cigarette. It was she now who sat on the arm of the leather chair.

My father said, "You're looking well, Lisbeth. You look like you're putting on some weight."

She looked even more annoyed and said, "Don't be ridiculous. This is a wool Chanel suit. I'm not putting on weight at all."

"Oh," he replied.

There was silence.

Then he said, "What have you done to your hair?"

"What do you mean?" she asked.

"What kind of color is that? It doesn't look natural."

Then he'd turn to Etienne and say, "I can't understand why women dye their hair to look unnatural. Nobody has orange hair like that."

"Gerald, this is ridiculous," she said.

Etienne laughed at the absurdity of it and perhaps with some vicarious pleasure at my father taking the inviolable on.

Then my father tried a doomed initiative. "What do you think of your daughter? Growing up to be quite pretty. She's good in school too."

"Yes," she answered.

"Everyone remarks on how precocious she is," he'd say.

"Yes," she replied dully, clearly uninterested in this turn of conversation.

"How's your job going?" he asked.

"Very well."

Even he could see she didn't want to talk to him. So now he'd turn his attention to what he really felt comfortable with, the problems of another man.

"Etienne, what do you think of this French Canadian business? Do you people really think it's any good to secede? You'll lose all your Canadian benefits if the province goes off on its own."

"Etienne," my mother said, "is a member of the French Liberation party. Obviously he thinks it's a good idea to secede. If you read the news, Gerald, you would know that."

My father ignored her.

Etienne said to my mother, "I support Levesque, Darling. I'm not in the French Liberation party. You should read the newspapers yourself."

"Well I can't stand," she said, "all this anglophone, francophone business. They should all get off the phone."

Etienne cringed.

"Well anyway," my father said thoroughly pleased, "you'll neverget everyone to agree to secede."

Etienne said, "Oh I wouldn't be so sure, Gerald."

My father looked over at me, having accomplished his mission of creating general unease. He could not care less about French Canadian politics. Who cares about a tin pot province? he'd say. They talk about their culture. What culture, he'd roar.

"Well I should be going," he said standing up.

My mother and Etienne both looked relieved, and slightly agitated.

"Yes," she agreed.

"Where's your things?" he said to me.

I ran off to get my scruffy suitcase, one of his. I returned and hovered about the entrance to the living room, holding the case, waiting for him. I was already wearing my beige duffel coat that was a bit dirty, I suddenly noticed.

"Say goodbye to your mother," he said.

I walked back into the living room toward her and she leaned slightly forward for a kiss, and I'd sort of miss her face and say, "Goodbye. Thank you for having me. It was very nice."

"It was, wasn't it, dahling?"

"Yes." I had rather enjoyed listening to her records when she and Etienne were out, and going through her closets and drawers looking for clues. Here's what I learned: she kept her clothes immaculately, very orderly. Her closets and drawers were stuffed. She was very neat, very conscientious, at least in that area. This did not tell me much but it was a start.

I wondered, as I nearly kissed her, about her musty smell, a smell her perfume did not cover up. A smell that was strong which either she woke up with or sometimes got in the afternoon. I didn't like the smell.

Etienne would boom, "See you in a month," and I'd say, "Yes thank you very much." My father and I would shuffle out of there, two ungainly people, one towering over the other, leaving the magazine cover people to their dinner and glass apartment high over the city.

Almost before we left the building, I imagined my mother and Etienne watching the city light up like opening night, the snow settling like angel raiment on the Henry Moore sculptures on Sherbrooke Street, alighting on the surrounding buildings' green limestone rooves, gently covering the gleaming cars parked silently on the street. I imagined them playing chess together, my mother wearing a black evening dress with lace sleeves. They always became more glamorous once I left.

That's because my father and I were now driving in the sleet, to his favorite bar, which was a bit out of the city, since everyone knows that drinks are cheaper a little out of the city. I didn't conjure up any angel raiment landing on these dark pot-holed rural roads bordered by closely set pastel-colored bungalows. I looked out the car window and heard my father say, "She's got no sense of humour, your mother."

I had just read the *Wreck of the Hesperus* and I saw a giant albatross flying behind the car with the alternating faces of Lisbeth or my father.

I looked out at the flat roads and wondered what was wrong with both these people I was relegated to. How many hours, if I added it up, until I was sixteen and I could leave. Too many to add up.

"What did you do with her?" he asked.

"We went to the Ice Capades. Half of it."

"Why half?"

"She got bored."

"Typical. It's because she wasn't the main attraction."

I sighed.

"What did you eat there?"

"She and Etienne went out Saturday night. They ordered in chicken for me."

"Kind of them. Who took care of you?"

"No one. They said it's safe because they have a doorman. Maybe they told him to look out for me."

"What if there'd been a fire?" he said.

"I guess the doorman would have come."

"Ridiculous," he said. "Can't she spend ten minutes with you?"

"Well I don't care if she doesn't spend time with me. It's difficult with her—"

We were now at the Cavalier Bar and it was as if he flew out of the car to the bar's double glass doors and Jeanette looked more happy to see me than my mother ever did and she mixed my father a scotch and soda even before we had got to the bar and a coke with lots of cherries for me.

I climbed up onto the barstool and she said, "How is your mother?" which made me know he had stopped in there for a scotch and soda or two on the way to pick me up, and I said, "Fine, she's on television you know." He said, "Amazing anyone would want to watch her. Couldn't give a damn about her own daughter."

That's when Jeanette said, "You shouldn't say that in front of her."

"Why the hell shouldn't I say anything? She knows what's going on, don't you darling?"

"Yes."

I'd watch carefully to see if Jeanette would continue this renegade development of bringing some gentleness into our lives. She was wringing out a cloth in the bar sink and bending over. Her gold heart shaped necklace was shaking as she scrubbed the side of the gray sink. Grey light. Purple lipstick.

"Ger-ald," she'd say in a French accent, "nobody likes to hear her maman insulted."

"Nobody has a mammon like Jacqueline does."

He could never pronounce French. Just "L'addition, s'il vous plait."

She straightened up and her white blouse looked shiny gray in the low bar light. "She needs a feeling of 'ome."

I was jumping up and down inside, as I sat stock still, waiting.

I did need something home-like, what was he, crazy?

"Nonsense," he bellowed out. "She's perfectly happy. Look at how she's always smiling, always laughing."

I am?

"Take her to a movie," she said, "or shopping." This I didn't like so much. Dragging around shops with my father. Instead of a dress, he might buy me batteries for my radio.

He lit a cigarette. I smiled shyly at Jeanette. "He's kind of a stuck mountain," I explained. "Mount Royale," I said to amuse myself.

She winked at me. "Dynamite 'im," she said.

Some man I hadn't noticed at the end of the bar said, "She will. Eventually. They all do."

My father smiled to his drink. "Absolutely true."

"What are we doing tonight?" I asked quickly, not interested in this conversation. I was never going to be the dynamiting type, I thought, not knowing I was building up a huge internal armory, just sitting there quietly.

"We'll have a few drinks here," he said, "and then go out for dinner and stop in for a quick one at that bar near the house. What do you think? You'd like that, wouldn't you?"

"I have homework to do."

"What homework?"

"I'm supposed to write a book report."

"On what?"

"*Little Women.*"

He pulled a couple of bar napkins from the square plastic holder. He pulled his gold ballpoint from his breast pocket and pushed the cap to have the ink come out. "Here," he said, "write your book report."

* Six

In my late teens I left my father and moved to Boston alone. I quickly got jobs as a waitress—in airports, hotels, and coffeeshops. I was comfortable in bars. The lighting, the staff, the clientele were, let's face it, home to me.

Women with teased hair and bartenders with coughs and self deprecating smiles fed me, told me what doctors to see, made sure I was not alone on Christmas eve.

But in an effort to "move up," I soon got a job as a secretary in a real estate finance company. The handsome president with his Rolex watch and enormous desk in a glass office stared at my breasts during the interview and agreed to pay me a $100 a week. Aside from typing all his correspondence, I typed out the daily contents of his wine cellar and a daily to-do list for his wife. He frequently reported to us as he arrived in the morning how much his wife weighed that day. (She kept her figure fastidiously so it was with pride he kept us up-to-date on these critical statistics.)

I lived in a studio apartment without a phone in a not yet gentrified area. It was all I could afford. One night I got mugged and some kids took my last forty dollars. The Pakistani cab driver passing by helped me. He was studying at Harvard and was the son of the Pakistan Ambassador to Vienna. I became involved with him for a short time and he wrote me forty-page letters, singing my praises, and bought me a dress from Albert Nipon.

His father told him that "waitresses were good at it" but I don't know if this has been empirically proven. Anyway, I never stayed with him. I spent some time as I did with anyone who came my way, as if they too were characters in a bar, this bar being the bar of the world.

Mostly though, in those years, and even later, I read a lot and seemed to have, as I've mentioned, lots of friends and men I obsessed about, most of whom I can't remember at all now.

I took pleasure in losing myself in work and, after my boss noticed how much I liked to work, he decided to teach me how to be a real estate finance saleswoman. He thought the real estate developers whom he sold to would be more willing to meet with a very young woman than a typical business man. The tax lawyers who wrote the partnership agreements called me Mata Hari.

Looking back, I wonder if the men I did business with thought they could pull a fast one on me. I was clearly not a businesswoman. I was a lure.

My boss was pleased, because I did attract some jobs, which he himself closed. The boss was shrewd and he knew, without my saying so, that this job was my first home that did not have alcohol at its center.

He and his vice president were kind to me, treated me as part of our motley small office, and we soon began to know each other's dreams, faults, and repetitions. I was inordinately loyal. I hadn't been "part of" before. And here I was being promoted. With a car and charge cards. He could smell how willing I was going to be.

Thus I flew all over the country promising men much money in return for equity in their low-income housing developments. I hardly understood what I was doing but I knew how to meet with men and I knew how to be undaunted.

I was rewarded with a secretary of my own, a slight increase in salary, and a brand new Volkswagen Rabbit. My Rabbit and I took frequent weekend trips to the sea.

I slept with men I met through my job, men I met travelling, men I met while doing my laundry, all of whom seemed to be slightly sad about their lives, insisting they wanted one thing in life (such as to own a hardware store) while they were living out the exact opposite (such as being a high paid business consultant). They would tell me their dreams as if I could maybe tell them how to make them come true. I nodded patiently and let them stroke my body.

Each day was work (where I wanted to be wanted and nurtured), talks with friends I picked up everywhere, drinks in softly-lit bars, walks up and down Newbury Street, Charles Street, the Charles River, music in jazz clubs or a rush seat at Symphony Hall, men's attention (where I wanted to be wanted and nurtured) and each day I waited to be rejected.

That was my talisman. I cried when my boss slighted me, when men were not addicted to me, when someone saw a flaw in me.

Otherwise I managed adroitly alone.

What had my mother been doing when she was the same age? She too, in her very early twenties, was working as a secretary, in London, where she had landed when she joined the RAF in Palestine. She told me later, and she told Canadians on her TV show, "I wanted to serve under the men who fly." Her face, she said, was on a British poster advertising the RAF. It was possible this was true, what with her quick eyes, her pert nose, her Audrey Hepburn prettiness.

Neither she nor I saw the point of attaining a university degree in our respective lives. We simply wanted the instant gratification of attention. We would stunningly make do by our wits.

Somehow, for different reasons, or were they the same, we were in a panic for someone to claim us.

She had many boyfriends, whom she slept with, as did I.

One of hers was a Bulgarian, my father said. The Bulgarian got her pregnant and she aborted. She lived in a basement flat that was simply "awful," he said.

I too was getting pregnant frequently. I would call the clinic while sitting at my desk for the result of the pregnancy test. I often didn't know who the father was. I would be eating dry toast as I was put on hold.

Within minutes, I would book an abortion. There was never any question. To have a child was an impossibility, an unhappy occurrence, an interruption. At that time, I did not give myself a chance to regret it. I could not see how I could take on someone else to care for. I never thought of trusting a man enough to take care of me.

In her mid twenties, my mother went to work for my father who was busy selling refrigeration. He was still married to a British Wren who, according to him, was institutionalized for madness. The Wren miraculously got better after she divorced my father.

I feared that same madness for myself if I had lived with my father into adulthood. What with the unkindness and disdain that came with his drinking.

So my father was in his forties, my mother in her twenties. She was his secretary. A pert, witty flirtatious Austrian. He squired her about. They went to the horse races in Paris. I think they both enjoyed over-stating themselves to each other and to whoever would listen. They had surmounted difficulties: she with moving about and losing countries and family. He in recovering from continual debts and demanding women.

My mother got pregnant by my father. And miscarried. She got pregnant again.

Was it that she had enough Jewishness in her to think it was good to have a child? Was it she thought my father could take care of her?

Did she not know she had no desire to be a mother? Was it that she was braver than me? One has a child, ignore the child, but one does it. One says that much of a yes to life.

But you don't attach to the child, you don't attach to the husband, you don't attach to anyone, you think about it, you try to, but you can't, because life, life will eventually break those attachments anyway.

Life, in short, can't be trusted so why bother pretending to your child that anyone is safe?

Life is treacherous and what better lesson for the child than to be the child's first treachery.

I too, in my early twenties began sleeping with my married real estate finance boss, but I did not run off with him, as my mother did with my married father. I simply ran off. Left the job. To be a poet, at least in lifestyle.

"Can't you make him fall in love with you?" my mother asked me on one of our visits when I was an adult. She was referring to my real estate finance boss.

"He would bore me," I said. I didn't want him. I wasn't sure how much I wanted myself.

That was our twenties. Different countries. Different mannerisms. Same themes. Was it simply the coincidence of our both being women? Or was it that she was inside me as I had been in her?

* Seven

When I was thirteen, my mother's career was at its height. She was on television weekly doing ironic short clips about the state of Canada, which somehow she always managed to tie into her love life. She spoke English and French perfectly, with that powerful intelligence of the out-sider, and the country got to listen to her equate Canadian indifference to a British Governor General to her own indifference to my British father. The country got to watch her on television equate the terrible uneasiness of Quebec's status in the Canadian union as akin to the current instability in her marriage to a French Canadian separatist.

The pure audacity of this, coupled with her Austrian old world way of dressing up in colored skirts and sleeves and her razor-like Austrian accent, made her intrinsically Canadian.

Canada, at that time, was the haven for sophisticated immigrants, people who snubbed their nose at the States or who couldn't get in, after all Canada was more socialist, hence enlightened, but not socialist enough to be repressive; just socialist enough to be broke, but then it looked like the States with all its wealth was going to end up that way too, so why not live in less commercial, less vulgar Canada?

She was also intrinsically Canadian in that she mixed European sophistication with a North American desire for stardom, attention. She was ambitious, or she must have been, to put these TV shows and these radio commentaries together. She wrote hundreds of letters to the editor that were published in the Montreal Gazette. She was recognized in the street, even with her big sunglasses.

We would be walking down Sherbrooke together, maybe for a Sunday afternoon coffee. She'd say as people passing by us glanced at her, "Do you see how they know me?"

One Saturday morning, I was dropped off downstairs at her apartment building early so my father could get to the bar on time, and she was asleep. Her apartment door was open, the bedroom door shut, so I played Spanish Duets with the Guitar or early Barbra Streisand on her record player, had a few cigarettes, and stared out the window.

At thirteen, I imagined myself as incredibly interesting doing this. Somehow I sensed Etienne was not there. He was either travelling on business or with his mistress. She had told me he had a mistress. She said it as if it was completely normal.

To entertain myself, I took the elevator up to the top of her apartment building and sat on the settees placed up there in a large room that one could rent for parties, and I talked to the apartment residents who came up to gaze at the view of Montreal. People remarked on St Joseph's Oratory, and Notre Dame de Grace, an exact replica of the one in Paris. Another church the exact replica of the Vatican. They would remark on the huge Canadian trees against the whitely blanketed streets.

Sitting there in the large room at the top, I met a French painter who wanted to paint me. I posed topless for him up there, thinking I was protecting myself from any untoward activities by refusing to go to his apartment. People walked in while he was hidden behind his easel, occasionally peering out at me, and they would shake their heads at this young half nude girl and this artiste who obviously was a fake without a studio.

I was not ashamed of my nudity. I simply thought the people who disapproved were not artistic like myself. I thought they were jealous that I was young and privy to such attentions. I did not suspect they might have lived through such attentions themselves and perhaps not had such a need for exhibitionism.

About noon I figured my mother was awake. I went down and she was just getting up, her short hair sticking up and she was wearing a very unglamorous terrycloth shapeless dressing gown, compared to her "outside" wear. She nodded hello to me, but with obvious annoyance at my being there which she tried to hide by looking for a cigarette, as she plugged in the kettle to boil some water.

I stood to the side, wanting to say something interesting and self-confident but instead hummed and bumped into her furniture and lit my own cigarette twice to get the light going.

She said, "What are you doing?" and I said, "I don't know" and then she padded back into her room for a long period while I wondered what to do next so I stared out the window and listened to more Streisand to distract me from the emptiness I felt from her rejection and then she came out, in jewelry and a cashmere sweater, elegant black slacks, and perfect make up, and then the buzzer rang and it was Jim Lawrence.

He stood at the door grinning, a black scarf jauntily wrapped round his neck. He was large and had an open face, and I had seen him on television. He was a news anchorman stationed in Toronto, but it turned out he lived in Montreal.

They decided to stay in for lunch, cold cuts which she happily put out on the Swedish table, asking him if he thought we looked alike, and he said, "A bit," and she said, "Everyone says so," but I could not imagine who that everyone was, except maybe people she asked in her own mind. I did not believe I looked like her. I was far too askew and passionate to look like a small coiffed woman who didn't have feelings.

Jim asked me about school and what I noticed about this show on television or that film, asked me as if I had very intelligent opinions, which soon had me responding very seriously, as if I were a station owner myself and these opinions were of great importance to him.

My mother smiled during my enthusiastic displays of sophistication and laughed uproariously when I pronounced pianist as "penis."

After lunch, they left to go to his apartment. I went back to the top of the building and took a swim in the indoor swimming pool that also had glass windows overlooking the city but from the pool you only saw the heavy ivory sky (there must be a sun hidden in there somewhere) from which snow would soon fall.

I went back downstairs and called the French painter and went back up to the top floor of the building so he could continue his work of painting and touching my breasts to move this way, that way, and did I know how beautiful I was, and could he kiss me just once, which was all very erotic, and I loved having my breasts touched, even though I knew I shouldn't, but I loved the insistence of it.

Needing a break from his attention, I said "Just a second," pulled on my blouse, and ran down to the apartment to make sure no one was home and had a quick cigarette and cognac down there, amazed at how I could make the best of any situation. Look at me! Etienne returned and said "Hello" in a remote, civilized tone. He did not even ask where she was. He got some things from their bedroom, and then he left.

I was sure he knew about Jim and I was sure she knew whatever there was to know about Etienne. They were at that stage where hurting each other was their remaining erotic connection.

It was 4 p.m., getting dark. The city began to light up and I went back upstairs to the painter, who was packing up, having given up on my flightiness, and perhaps going to meet his girlfriend or wife, I never knew, and then I went back down and looked through the Montreal Star for a movie playing nearby. The phone rang and it was Jim Lawrence, her boyfriend, "Are you alright?"

A man calling me.

"Yes," I said. "What do you think of my going to see *A Man and a Woman*? Is it any good?" I asked.

He said, "One moment" and he muffled something to her, perhaps suggesting that they join me and then he said, "Where is it playing?"

I said at the Place Vendome.

"What time?"

"7:10."

I heard him say to her, "We can do that another time," and then he said to me, "Okay, we'll meet you."

I stood in line and bought them tickets with my father's money. The Place Vendome was full of French couture shops and women in huge fur hats walking around holding their coats. They were attended by tall husbands holding credit cards. The floor of the Place Vendome was expensive fake cream marble with black diamonds in it and my heels clicked as if I was dancing as I walked along the main floor. (One had to walk quickly for the proper effect.) Above the Place Vendome were very expensive large modern apartments, in which a Chinese girl in my school lived.

Jim and my mother arrived at the theatre and she seemed a bit sheepish, embarrassed. Here was her daughter, who was now showing up everywhere.

My mother politely thanked me for the tickets.

Jim looked exuberant, and said, "Imagine being out with two beautiful women."

In the movie house, she relaxed and stroked my hair and remarked that it was a nice cut, layered like that. "Does she look like me?" she asked Jim again.

He turned to me, his eyes dancing, and winked at me. "A little," he said.

"I can't see it," she said.

He got up to get popcorn for me. She asked me if I liked him. "Yes," I said, "he's very sexy." Her eyes darted toward me for a second. "Well he is," I said.

"Yes," she said, "You're right. Funny you would notice. He thinks you're very nice also."

I was pleased that someone on her side liked me.

"I went swimming this afternoon," I ventured.

"What did you wear?" she asked.

"I borrowed one of your swimsuits."

"Oh."

Jim returned.

My mother seemed to steal glances at me, with a worried look which I interpreted to mean that she was beginning to sense I was not a weakling or someone, like every other woman, she could dismiss.

She took some of the popcorn and then he handed me the box.

"She should watch her figure," my mother said about me.

I was offended, for this was to say my figure's flaws were worthy of watching, something I was beginning to worry about myself. What if I ended up overweight and bald like my father?

"What did you do this afternoon?" he asked me.

"I swam. A man upstairs is painting me."

"He is?" she asked. "Who?"

"A Frenchman on Floor 12, I think."

"Is it in the nude?" she laughed for Jim's amusement.

I was shocked at how easily she wanted me to be the butt of a joke.

"Sort of," I said.

"What do you mean by sort of?" Jim asked.

"I'm half nude."

She looked at me strangely and then laughed. "Well you do seem to entertain yourself." What could she possibly mean by that and what other possible choice did I have but to entertain myself, but all that happened was that she reached her hand out languorously and rested it on Jim's chest.

Of course I entertain myself.

✳ Eight

My father used to say to me, "Put on something nice," which meant the knit skirt and top that he had bought me, after he'd asked a woman he had seen in a restaurant where she got that "lovely suit."

So I would get dressed, add some pink lipstick, and then he would take me to an elegant French restaurant where there was as much silverware per place setting as there was in Eaton's windows. He would hold out my chair for me, light my cigarette and then I would hear his disembodied voice from behind his big menu, "What would you like, Darling?"

We were sitting thus at lunch at La Tour Eiffel when I noticed him watching someone at the doorway of the restaurant dining room with unusual intensity. His eyes lit up and his cheeks gained unusual healthy color.

I looked to the door and there was Etienne, my mother's husband, with a small blonde woman wearing a pale tweed blue and white suit with many strings of pearls round her neck, a woman who seemed more gentle than my mother. They were led by the maitre d' to a romantic corner table.

As Etienne passed our table, he espied the "old mad Brit," as he called my father. No doubt he couldn't miss him since my father's enthusiasm lit up his face as if he had just won the Olympic Gold Medal. Etienne said, "Hello Gerald, How nice to see you."

I was slighted by Etienne's ignoring me. Didn't he know that I couldn't possibly have any loyalty to my mother?

"I knew it was only a matter of time," my father said to me, "before that whole mess would unravel. I told him when he married her that it would never work. She could never be faithful."

"But Etienne's also being unfaithful."

"She probably drove him to it."

"What do you mean?"

"Your mother is the type who is very amusing for a little bit and then it's absolutely awful."

"Jim Lawrence, her lover, seems to like her."

"For now," my father responded.

I turned my head toward Etienne who was looking quite tall and elegant himself, his head tilted and smiling, listening to this quietly talking woman.

"Well everybody does it," my father said, when I asked him about men being unfaithful.

"Even people who are in love?" I continued, with teenage fervor.

"It's hard to stay in love. Maybe people in England like my family are faithful. I don't think my brother ever cheated on Eileen, but perhaps that is lack of imagination."

I noted happily that the waiter couldn't take his eyes off me as he took away the turbot.

My father was scribbling something onto the back of his business card.

"What are you doing?"

"I'm writing Etienne a note so he won't worry that either of us will say anything to Lisbeth."

"What does it say?"

He handed it to me, his eyes happy at this rare opportunity for true creativity.

I read, "Hear no evil. See no evil. Speak no evil."

I handed it back to him thinking it was a bit of a cliché but maybe this was how men spoke to each other.

My father handed the card to the waiter and pointed to Etienne.

The waiter officiously walked it over and Etienne read it and looked back toward my father and lifted his wine glass to him in appreciation.

"There, that's done," my father said.

"Do you think Etienne loves that woman?" I asked my father.

"How would I know?"

He looked over at her surreptitiously. "She looks quite nice," he said.

"Can you tell from looking?" I asked.

"You can tell nothing. A lot of people know how to seem like they are in love when they're not and a lot of people don't seem in love when they are."

"What type are you?"

"I don't know." I thought he might be in love with the list of cognacs he was studying.

My father took off his glasses and ordered one of his true loves. "Do you want anything?" he asked.

"No thanks. Do you think Lisbeth would care that he's here with another woman?"

"I doubt it," he said. "She doesn't care about much. I thought you said she already knows about this woman."

"Yes. But do you think she would care?"

"Your mother doesn't care about anything except herself."

"Daddy, answer a question with a complete answer," I said impatiently.

"What do you want to know exactly?"

I started to tear up a bit. "I don't know." What I wanted was to hear something I hadn't heard before. To not be condemned to this little box of repeated dismissals. "I don't know exactly," I whined.

"So it seems."

"I want to know," I said flushed and teary on wine perhaps, and the imminent sentence of growing up into such a grown up world, "I want to know," I said, "if anybody cares about anything."

"Of course people care about things. People care about lots of things. It's just that those things change."

✳ Nine

My mother was living alone now. Etienne had moved out. Jim was still around as well as Alvin, a meek small writer, who paid breathless homage to her and with whom she spent time when Jim was on assignment. She was somewhat disdainful of Alvin and I suspect didn't like sleeping with him. When he called in his earnest high voice, she asked me to say that she wasn't well, you know, it was that time. She seemed to have her period three weeks out of a month.

And there was also Andy who was only 24 and who worked in TV like she did and was very ambitious and in later years I thought that he had pursued her to help his career. He was short and always speaking loudly and posturing and gesticulating and was more effervescent than I was. She bought a television set for him, which she and I delivered in her Peugeot. She carried it in to him while I waited in the car.

There were others, too.

Jim Lawrence remained the most interesting to me because he was taller and stylish and talkative and liked to laugh.

"What is everyone doing today?" he asked one morning as I sat bizarrely in one of her knit dresses. I was about fourteen.

"Well she is here," my mother said. "And I want to go over to Sonia Rykiel, there is a sale. Jim darling do you want to come?"

He looked at me. "What are you doing?"

"I don't know. I think I'll stay here," I said.

I didn't like excursions with my mother. She was impatient with me and didn't like the way I walked or what I pointed at to show her in the store. I didn't like that she wouldn't introduce me to anyone that she ran into. I didn't like that she would think nothing of spending thousands of dollars on clothes for herself but would want me to pay for my own lunch. Sometimes she paid but more often than not, I reached for my money, like my father would, quickly, so as not to be rejected. I would take the check and she wouldn't even thank me. She would act as if I were a fool, which I was.

"I'll probably go for a swim."

"I'll go with Jacqueline," Jim said.

"If you like . . ." she said.

I was a little surprised at his choosing to spend time with me, but then wouldn't anyone given a choice between she and myself? I could see where he would select the more pleasant option. She must drive him nuts.

I went to look for one of her bathing suits as she began putting on one of her fur coats. She took the keys from the entryway table and said, "I'll see you both in an hour." However, we followed her out and she pressed the Down button for the elevator and we pressed the Up to the swimming pool.

"Swimming is how I keep so young," she said to Jim, as we waited for our respective elevators.

He nodded, smiling.

"It's not how I keep young," I said.

The swimming pool was at the top of her building and I went to the windows and looked down at the city. Montreal seemed to still be climbing up the mountain it was built on. Standing there, I looked at all the empty spaces filled with snow and black telephone lines amid the different buildings and sloping streets and difficult-to-walk-on cobblestones, and I thought this is still a pioneer city. The settling is still going on. The city is still young.

I said to myself, but not in words, all of it, all of it I will conquer.

I turned back to the pool and Jim said, "I just realized I don't have any trunks."

"What about your underwear?"

He looked around. "There's no one up here. How about in the nude? Do you mind?"

I shook my head, of course not. After all, what did he think? That I was a child and would be offended by this show of bohemianness?

But even if I admired such self-assured free-spiritedness on his part, I wasn't going to let him see my own overflowing body. It was one thing to be half nude with some man I would never see again, but another thing to be compared in any way to her. I would stay in her 1950s Givenchy gold one piece bathing suit that made me look like some kind of stage scenery.

I turned to go down to the other end of the pool where I began carefully walking down the black step rails into the water, carefully, as if it might hurt me, when I heard a loud threatening splash from the other end and there was Jim flying through the water. He seemed to instantly be down at my end, where I was gingerly getting used to the water temperature. I could see his buttocks as he charged by. He touched my end of the pool and then turned around to swim to the other length.

He shook his head and pushed water out of his lungs, like a snorting seal, when he stopped at the other end for air, and said, "Nice isn't it?" I said, "Yes," as I swam quietly along.

"Do you like my mother a lot?" I asked doing the breaststroke.

"I like your mother, yes."

"What do you like about her?"

His green eyes looked over at me. "I like that she is her own person. She's smart and she's . . . " he was searching . . . "incisive. She's charming, too. She's tough."

"I see." I was stumped on the "charming" word.

"She's very funny too."

She is?

"She's a survivor. When you think that she lost her family in Europe. The war. She's made a successful life here."

"She didn't lose her family. Her mother's still alive," I said, not looking at him.

"But she never lived with her mother," he said from the other end. He was no longer in motion, and had both arms splayed out on the side of the pool.

"Did she tell you this?" I asked. I wondered if my mother had been dramatizing, but, as I wondered this, I felt my father's voice speaking inside me.

"Who else would have?"

"True," I said.

I had to concentrate on all this. I had heard this version, as you know, from my father. But I was cross-referencing. I didn't trust my father's version. I was also busy concentrating on not looking at Jim under the water. What did all that equipment do when submerged like that?

I went back to thinking about her. I tried to feel sorry for her, which was difficult since I spent so much time feeling sorry for myself.

"You have a different nature," he said.

"I do?"

"You're more gentle."

"Yes."

I was breaststroking away from him so I wouldn't have to fight looking at the seaweed of him under the water.

"You both hurt all the time," he said, "but you show it differently. But what's interesting," he said to himself, "is that you're both hurt in the same ways."

She hurt? How could she with her dismissive eyes and cruel tone of voice be hurt?

Another man fooled by her.

It seemed only a few minutes later, after some silent laps on both our parts and me thinking maybe then the answer was to try harder with her, be more understanding, more loving, since she apparently is hurt, then if I'm loving, maybe something good would happen between us, when Jim asked what I thought of a certain movie that was playing and I asked if Toronto was really as dull as everyone said. I thought about how my father didn't like that I was half Jewish, didn't want me raised as a Jew and how my mother never mentioned she was Jewish, even though I knew it from her.

I swam some more, while Jim was busy doing laps as if trying out for some competition, and I breaststroked away while going over the fact she was motherless too, and it was this strange reality that we had in common.

I swam and thought what does it mean to come from a line of mothers who don't want to be mothers, instead they want to be women just living and if truth be told that is what I want to be, a woman being a woman, and then Jim got out of the water while I was swimming the other way and then I got out of the water at the other end and he came down and handed me a towel, now that he had his trousers on and then he held the door for me as we turned to go back down to her apartment.

The next day, while she waited for Jim to return, I asked her a question. I ventured it from the other couch. "Did your mother leave you?" I asked.

She snapped her cigarette lighter. "Why would she have done that? Of course not."

She got up and walked out of the room, her feet clicking on the polished wood floor.

✳ Ten

I was sitting at the Bistro by myself pretending to read *Portnoy's Complaint*, a book I carried around to assure everyone of my fifteen-year-old artistic intelligence.

The Bistro is on Mountain Street, next to a crepe restaurant where visiting female tourists go and swear they won't eat that much sugar again. The bistro is also next to The Rainbow Bar and Grille, a discotheque where people allegedly would sight Leonard Cohen and his leggy blondes all the time. The Rainbow Bar and Grille was next to an expensive furrier with a plain window and the same lustrous coat hung as advertisement for four years. I never saw anyone go in or out of the shop. I went to the Bistro all the time, as you know, but I did not go to the Rainbow Bar and Grille because somehow I knew I was not in the showgirl league that attracted the famous bard of sultry words. I stuck to the Bistro where I received my own brand of lesser attention.

So I was in the Bistro when Mort Amber sat down next to me. He sat down and said, "You know I don't really know you, but I see you everywhere down here. You have an interesting face. What's your name?"

I said, "Jacqueline. I know who you are, I've seen your film on television."

Immediately he sat up a little taller.

"Did you like it?" he asked.

"I did. It was very good," (although I couldn't remember it. I only remembered his name for some reason. I think I had heard other people talking about him.) "What are you filming now?" I quickly shifted to something I was not expected to know.

I was not attracted to Mort, a man probably in his thirties with a dark beard and earnest eyes. I could tell by the way he so intently cocked his head when he was listening to me that this was a man who would really want to know a woman, and I didn't want to be known. I wanted men to spread their fingers and desire wide so I could artfully slip through and away while they were smiling at me. Mort was the kind of man who wanted you to focus on him and thus hold you down. Maybe I was wrong. Maybe he knew someone who knew someone who knew someone who might see whom I really was. And then I could stop slipping through fingers.

He talked about his next film, an Eskimo anthropological film that sounded like the worst of Canadian earnestness, so I concentrated on the soft music playing while I nodded and watched the waiters wait for their drinks at the bar and watched the Frenchmen watching me and then I heard him say, "Want to come to a party?"

"Where?"

"In Westmount."

Why not? I thought. Be different to go where people didn't have to pay for drinks.

I got into his small neat car, a car of a man following a pattern to his life, who watches his gas bill assiduously, at this point I thought him a complete bore, he was still droning on about the Eskimo film that he had been working on for the last eight years.

We had left the downtown area of the bars and were now in Westmount, where the English live. Where the big houses are. Where the apartment buildings look like houses.

He parked the car.

A woman in a fringed shawl and long skirt welcomed us and took my yellow coat. Underneath I had my usual revolutionary garb, a black velvet jumpsuit that I had worn so much it had stretched beyond my ankles and dragged in the snow so the cuffs were torn and yellow from street salt. I wore a brown leather belt slung around my hips.

"Drinks are over there," and she pointed us to a makeshift table. "Mort, I'll get something for you," I said. I wanted to get away from him. He looked like he was seeing a lot of people he knew. He said, "Fine, anything" and I raced over and reached past the wine bottles to the hard stuff. I poured a scotch straight for me and poured him a red wine.

I walked back, handed him the wine, which he accepted, smiled thanks and bent his head down closer to some small woman with no makeup who was intently telling him about her film.

I turned to the back of the house and saw the lights in the owner's back garden. The fir trees were lit up with white Christmas lights, even though it was no longer Christmas, and the patio furniture was covered in snow. I turned to go back to the makeshift bar, just for the security of being near it, and then I suddenly heard a raspy Austrian voice.

I looked through the arched opening between the rooms and there she was, standing small and tight in an intimate crowd of admirers. I could see the charms of her bracelet, her slingback shoes, the shimmer of her stockings. I heard her voice and then I heard her laugh in quick agreement with herself. I saw her small quick head look round at her audience for applause.

I didn't know what to do. I had the same feeling David must have felt when he saw the foot of the Goliath.

I looked back to Mort and he was smiling very understandingly to the young filmmaker. "Yes, Yes," I heard him say, "I've had that problem too. I understand exactly," and he boomed out a laugh.

I walked over to Mort and he quickly looked at me, but with slight confusion in his eye, why had he brought this fifteen-year-old anyway? He didn't acknowledge my hovering about so I turned to another room, not the one my mother was in, and there were other clusters of people and their eyes turned questioningly to me too, Oh a new person, and then dropped away, for what can a fifteen-year-old have to say?

Now I was in a doorframe and on my right was my mother's cluster.

I took a big swig of my drink. Oh lessen this pain, this pain of constant unworthiness of love.

"Is that you, Jack?" I heard.

I turned and it was Andy, her infant boyfriend. He always called me Jack, instead of Jackie. I resented this familiarity.

"What are you doing here?" he asked.

"I don't know."

"Your mother's over there."

"I see."

"Would you like to be introduced?" he asked.

"No."

"Oh come," he said, "you might have a lot in common."

"We've been introduced before and we didn't find that much in common. It makes conversation difficult."

"Maybe she won't remember you," he said, laughing.

I looked intently at him. Was he tipping me off?

"Maybe not," I said.

"Lisbeth," he yelled out. "There's someone I want you to meet." His hands were already at the base of my back pushing me towards her crowd.

"Lisbeth de Bellefeuille," he said. "This is Jacqueline, a lovely girl. A little offbeat. A little untamable, a little angry maybe but a young girl nonetheless."

"Hello," she said. "How did you get here?"

"I came with Mort."

"A terrible filmmaker," she said.

I didn't respond. Already I had come with the wrong crowd.

"Do you go out with him?" she asked.

"No."

"Are you still a virgin?"

"Lisbeth, this might not be the right moment—" Andy said, laughing.

"Why not?" she replied to him.

"I am," I said.

Nobody in her circle knew what to make of this little chat, including me.

"You should get rid of it," she said to me. "You're getting hung up."

"Right now?" Andy asked.

"No," she laughed, "I mean in general. Who wants to be a virgin?"

They all laughed, but at what? Just then she put her hand on a man's arm as he lit her cigarette. She exhaled the smoke while looking at me.

I said, "I just remembered, I have to go," and turned to the bar to get another drink.

"Not so fast," Andy said, putting a strong arm on my shoulder.

Suddenly the people around my mother had disappeared. While I was registering that, Andy moved off too. I wondered if I had brought an ill wind or if this was their happy chance to leave her and find other people. My mother and I were left alone. I looked out again through the back windows.

"Nice house isn't it," I said.

She looked away, embarrassed. She hated small talk.

"Who are you here with?" I asked.

She said, "I came with Sydney." (Sydney was her boss at the Film Board, which made me wonder about my father's edict that she slept her way to the top.) "But of course," she continued, "I had forgotten his wife is here."

"Which one?"

She nodded toward a pleasant looking woman, a motherly type, someone I might like for a mother, a plump and earnest looking woman in a white shirt tucked into a simple skirt, who seemed to be making the effort of kindly listening to the other woman she was talking to.

"Does she know?" I asked.

"I don't know," my mother responded and then surprisingly giggled like we were two friends.

Encouraged, I said, "Are you going home with him to your place?"

She switched back to her usual personality and said, "Don't be ridiculous."

I struggled for something interesting to say, but nothing came to me. What did we have to talk about? I scanned my mind.

"Mort is a bore, I agree," I said.

"Terrible," she replied. She was looking about and not at me.

"Well I better go."

"Of course," she said in a tone that indicated that I was always going, and stared off round the room for other people.

When I realized outside that I didn't have enough money for a taxi and so I would have to walk downtown where not having money wouldn't matter because someone always bought me a drink at the Churchill Pub, I trudged along in the shoveled out street walkways, feeling wounded, and not sure why. I felt cold. Not from the weather, in those years, I was used to such weather, it was part of living from bar to bar to have your ears red and hurting, and your feet cold, and in Montreal, you map out all the underground pathways to make your way to the Churchill Pub or the Bistro.

I wasn't cold from the frigid Montreal night, because I knew I would get to an underground walkway soon, near a subway stop, which would take me to a walkway to the next subway stop. I was cold from knowing I was not close enough to her to ask her for money for a taxi. I was not close enough to her to say, Why don't we have dinner sometime, just the two of us and I'll ask you what it means to grow up to be a woman. Should I be like you, I would ask her, or Sydney's wife? I was not close enough to her to know what it was about me that was so disappointing.

The heat rushed into me as I pushed in the door of the Winston Churchill pub. The bar was crowded so I made my way to a wooden corner table and sat down, finally safe. A green lawyer's lamp hung down so low that it hit my head.

Jarringly, and suddenly, I heard a British voice, "Hello there. My name's Freddie Seebolm."

A hand with long bony fingers stuck out under the lamp.

Above him was the bar portrait of Winston Churchill whose portliness and self-confidence in the portrait reminded me of my father.

I put my head to the side of the lamp and there on the other side of the wooden table was a young blonde man with a thin face and a look of disarray which was quite pleasant to me, an obvious rebel, and he said, "I'm at McGill. Are you?"

This was enormously flattering since I was still in high school. I began to cheer up.

I noticed his blue jacket, like a prep school boy, his expensive white shirt, his bad boy too long blonde hair. His face was thin and sinister but his eyes were tired and kind. Almost too old for a young man's.

"No."

"A French college?" he asked.

"No. I'm English speaking."

"Well, so am I."

"Yes. The accent would indicate that."

"Well tell me something about yourself," he said.

"I'm not that interesting. "

"Well," he said, "there's an unusually self-aware answer."

"You asked."

"Are you hoping to meet interesting people here? Get the moves down? Imitate them to get out of your rut?" he asked.

I peered my head round the lamp.

"Yes," I lied. "Now tell me something about yourself."

"I come from a wealthy family in England and I'm here to waste my time. At McGill. Which I don't like."

"Why?"

"I'm not the studious type. I'm bound to be thrown out any time now."

Further proof he was a rebel and possibly meant for me. Not to mention being English, of the master race who saved me from my mother.

I liked him too much to ask him to buy me a drink. So I flashed my eyes round the room hoping someone would catch them, be intrigued and then send me a drink. It usually worked. I circled the room once, twice and aha, there was a taker, a man with a ponytail, dressed in a Sergeant Pepper's jacket. He smiled at me and motioned with his hand. I nodded. He turned back to the bar. The bartender looked over at me, once Sgt. Pepper pointed me out. He handed Sgt. Pepper a cognac.

Now I would get warm.

Freddie Seebolm was simply looking about him, holding his beer, and not seeing anyone.

I started giving him darting pouty stares that usually got a man's attention.

These were not working.

Then I saw a woman who always sat at the same table. She was probably in her fifties; although I thought anyone over thirty was in her fifties. She had dark hair, long, badly cut so it looked thinner than it might have been, and she wore an attractive velvet maroon top. She looked "interesting." She used to always watch me with amusement. Even I knew she was seeing herself.

I waved to her.

She waved back.

I said, "Excuse me," to Freddie and went over to her table.

"Can I get you anything?" I asked, even though I had no money.

"No, no" she said. "Are you having a nice time with your young man?"

"I just met him. I don't think he's interested in me. I like him though. He's funny."

She said nothing.

"May I sit down?" I asked.

"Of course."

"You're here a lot," I said.

"I shouldn't be. I should leave these places to people your age but I don't."

This time it was I who said nothing.

"I think it's because," she said, "I enjoy the liveliness here. It cheers me."

"That's why I come too," I said.

"And to be looked at."

I blushed, thinking that this was a compliment.

"You will find," she said, "that imperceptibly they stop looking at you. Or desiring you. A day you just cross over that line. You have a long way to go before that, of course."

"Oh I'm sure men still desire you," I said, as if talking to my mother.

"I don't really care anymore," she said.

I nodded, seriously. I didn't believe her. Everyone wants to be desired. Wasn't that all of life?

"Are you an artist?" I asked.

"Does it matter?"

I shrugged. "I guess not."

But to me, it did. It seemed it must be the only reason to go on living. I didn't know why I felt that but I did. If you didn't have that, then you were too vulnerable to all the losses that can befall you. You would feel them without any hope.

She must be braver than me not to need that.

"Do you have a boyfriend?" I asked.

"I have a lover. He lives in Quebec City and comes most weekends. You will see him. I will bring him in. I am sure he will enjoy meeting you."

"Oh . . . that man over there has brought me a drink." Sergeant Pepper was holding a cognac looking for me. "I'll see you again," I said, "I'll pop over."

I got up and smiled at her, warmly, as if to say, hang on. Hang on.

I returned to my original table and a man who moved by me so quickly that I did not see him said, "Nice legs" and that brief contact gave me just an ounce, a tiny ounce, of courage.

Freddie nodded to me and Sgt. Pepper came and sat down next to me.

He told us he was Canadian, a photographer.

"Isn't this place kind of tired tonight. . . " he said.

Lord Seebohm on my right studiously listened to us.

"Well, I don't know—" I said.

"I'm going to watch the sun come up later from the top of the Mountain. Want to join me?" Sgt. Pepper asked.

I pondered for a second. I liked the idea of watching the sun come up over Mount Royale with this photographer. I liked the sort of picturesque picture of myself watching the sun come up. I liked the picture far more than I liked the reality of sitting bored out of my mind on the top of a cold mountain waiting for a sun to come up that might not even come up, while making conversation with this oddball with a ponytail, whom I suspected was gay and was only inviting me to prove to himself he wasn't. I would have preferred Lord Seebohm and his youthful nihilism. Maybe even talking to that strange woman.

I looked to see if Freddie Seebohm was going to pursue me.

He saw me look, lifted his drink, and said "Carry on then," which I knew to mean that he was one of those drinkers, one of those men, who wouldn't make the effort.

I would have to.

His true love was probably Guinness stout.

I stood up with the photographer and said, "Let's go." At least I knew where I would be staying tonight.

✳ Eleven

Like many lovers, my mother and Jim got an erotic charge from taunting each other about their dalliances. I'd hear her tease him about how stupid Valerie or Malka was. "But then you're not after good conversation," she'd say loudly, prodding him. He'd quickly come back, "Oh, that's not true at all," and then they'd stupidly laugh again.

I halfheartedly listened to them while playing jazz on her stereo. I didn't give their conversation much attention because obviously they were having it to kick-start something. I didn't know that then but I felt it.

He would be lying back in the corner of the white couch and she would be sitting next to him and then she'd be bending on her knees over him, both of them smiling, while playing at mock jealousy and anger and I would watch them from a far distance, as stoned and disappeared on an alto sax solo as if I were on heroin, travelling up and down on the aching notes and deeply felt bass while smiling daftly at them every now and then at inopportune moments, my mind dipping with the alto sax.

I looked out the window at Sherbrooke Street and saw the pointed green roofs with a cross on every eave of the French convent, looked further down to Atwater at the crowds starting to swarm around the Forum for the hockey game. I could see the crowds outside but I could also see the blustery silence of an icy cold day.

She'd then kiss Jim deeply, bend over him further, and he'd put his hands on her waist and their discussion fell off a bit and the feeling between them moved into a low alto sax of its own. Soon they were in the bedroom.

The sun went down and I heard low laughs from her in the bedroom as I turned the record over and listened to twenty minutes of Cannon-ball Adderly and eventually, when I had played every bearable record of hers I could bear, for she had a preponderance of muzak, Herb Alpert, Mantovani, stuff I put my nose up at, they'd emerge.

Jim smiled, a little tired, fully dressed as if he had just arrived, and she casual in a red cashmere sweater and black wool pants but without the commensurate jewelry and he asked me if I was hungry. She was smiling victoriously.

"You should get your daughter some new records," Jim said to her about me. "She is a jazz nut, even now."

My mother, surprisingly, laughed, as if he had said something witty.

"No, I mean it," he said.

She laughed again. Had she gone daft? I looked at her bristling round the coffeepot and I realized that she was something I rarely saw: She was happy.

Another time my mother and Jim took me with them to his place. Jim lived in an old Montreal granite townhouse with big bay windows on one of the streets that ran up the edge of Mount Royale. I went with them inside and he had two big rooms, with brown stuffed chairs and Persian frayed rugs.

I immediately went over to his records.

"You listen to Gentle Jugs?"

"Of course," he said. "Want me to put it on?"

I nodded.

My mother looked confused. She was always confused when I knew something.

All of a sudden Gentle Jugs' gentle sax rolled through the room, taking me into its gentle embrace and I felt softer, wilder, my spirit roaming round Jim's apartment. With the music sifting through my blood I became relaxed, kittenish. I had friends. I belonged some-where, with people who made music like this. I was not alone.

I looked at the sun coming in through his bay windows, and round the room for more clues to his sensuality and then I saw Jim looking at me. I thought he was seeing my spirit, that he saw I had found the key to harboring purity and beauty. I thought he saw that I was safe.

I smiled at him and he smiled back.

My mother was playing with the zipper of her fur jacket, "Jim dahling can you help me?"

He walked over to her and tried but he wasn't good with mechanical things. She got rough with it and said, "Oh forget it. I can see you can't do anything."

She wasn't hearing any music.

I was also someone who was not good with mechanical things so I didn't offer to help. Instead, I listened to the rolling music and let that music tell me in very sure sounds that, undoubtedly, I had a future after all. One of art and music and sensuality and rooms with frayed rugs and handsome men. I only had a few more years, I decided, before my future would come and claim me.

✳ Twelve

My mother, when she was in her thirties, married the French journalist whom she inspired to leave his wife and children. The same man I had seen her kissing when I was four. She took his very beautiful long aristocratic-sounding French last name, de Bellefeuille.

He was a French Canadian, serious about his nationality, and she had already lived in five countries—Vienna, Czechoslovakia, Palestine, England and Canada—and would never again to be serious about any nationality. He believed in political righteousness, she believed in irony. He was literal, she was practical. They apparently had nothing in common.

My mother and Etienne stayed together while Expo 67, the Montreal World's Fair, went on, and she could attend various balls as his wife, since she spoke many languages, and made a hit with all the ambassadors and delegations.

I remember seeing her once cross the street in a beautiful pale blue shimmering ball gown, delicately holding the skirt up as she crossed a puddle to a car to a party. She laughed with Halle Selassie and Lester Pearson.

She had Jim and many other men as lovers while married to Etienne. Etienne had that one woman I had seen him with at the restaurant with my father. Etienne's mistress was also married, Polish, and would not leave her husband till her son was older. Etienne waited faithfully for her and eventually married his mistress, once my mother and he finally divorced.

In her thirties, while married to Etienne, my mother also fell in love. But this time with a man more suited to her in personality. He was British, not Canadian. He was a successful humorist writer. For some odd reason, he was doing a job in Canada. Perhaps like all writers, he needed money. He looked like Rex Harrison and my mother looked a bit like a red headed Audrey Hepburn, which says something about the uncanny intuitiveness of movies.

Alan, like most men in her life, was married, but, unlike Etienne or my father who left their marriages for my mother, Alan would not leave his wife. He had five children. We all gleaned from this that he was decent.

But they were definitely in love. His picture was all over her apartment. His books. She talked of nothing else. How brilliant he was. How good in bed. How perfect for her. How witty.

They met in her office at the National Film Board, where she was a film producer. It was hard for me to imagine her collaborating with people at her work but even then I knew that was my own deficiency. I viewed her entire life through her deficiencies as a mother. I admired that somehow she was good at work but I could not imagine how someone so self-centered could come up with ideas. I could not imagine her having the patience one needs for work, but she was Austrian with a Germanic temperament. She was efficient. She liked striking tasks off her list. And whatever idea she came up with, she liked. She would hold meetings with agendas on purple paper, her lavender sheets, she said. Everything was sexual innuendo.

She kept being promoted which my father, as you know, attributed to her sleeping with her bosses. And indeed she did sleep with most of her bosses. But even then I knew that was not how she got promoted. My mother was clever. Clever with her scripts for television and clever about being a "character" in a government institution like the Film Board. It was not a demanding job, but a secure job. She was European and that was vaguely alluring to Canadians. She was sophisticated and did not give a damn about convention, which was alluring to artists.

She, like her countryman, Freud, thought everything was to do with sex and she was not shy about seeing a world that functioned through the prism of her flirtations. The hapless Canadian men she met were in heaven.

I did not realize that the Film Board, since it was her only real job ever, was the family she never had. She always said that, but I refused to hear it, for obvious reasons.

Anyway Alan, her true love, this British writer, was introduced to her in her office, as many writers were. The man who introduced them thought they would have much in common. After all, she had lived in England and liked the wit and the cold heartedness and so, once they met, they spoke about where she had lived, about where he lived, and since Etienne was away for the summer, my mother offered to show Alan Montreal.

European graciousness.

My mother and Alan proceeded to live together in her apartment for the next two months, while Etienne was in South America. Once when I was about thirteen, I walked in on them. They were making love on the stairs to her bedroom. All three of us were embarrassed at my interruption and I turned and ran back downstairs and quickly left.

She not only showed him Montreal, but she showed him Canada and she took him to Hollywood to meet the few contacts she had there, Canadian or European émigrés who had gone after more than the Canadian film industry.

Alan had worked with Terry Thomas, Peter Sellers, was educated at Oxford in economics. He, like my mother, was not interested in what it was to be hurt. They abhorred what was serious. Their entire relationship was commenting on each other's sentences. Who could make the wittier remark. They laughed all the time together.

At dinner one night, seated with many people, my mother was placed far away from Alan. Alan turned to his agent and said, "I have only loved two women in my life."

And he heard from the other end of the long table the deep Austrian raspy voice, "Who was ze ozther one?"

When I went to visit her, she would parade around naked, in and out of her bath, and tell me that Alan loved her breasts.

They wrote feverish transatlantic love letters, since it was before the time of email. Every Christmas he called her and said he was having a terrible time without her.

I thought the success of their love affair was the distance. If only he knew, I thought, who she really is.

In my thirties, I too, fell in love. I was living by the sea, hiding from growing up, trying to heal my craven longing for love with sea-beauty. It's odd, my mother said, how you live like someone retired while I'm the one having a career.

The man I fell in love with was an orphan and I fell in love with our mutual fate of loneliness. He was a carpenter and anti-capitalistic, anti-bourgeois and, most strikingly, anti-ambition, and I pledged myself to our outsider status. In his complete unworldliness, I thought I was safe from the aggressive hurting of my mother.

The carpenter and I lived together and it took years before we had a common language. Even if I wanted to forget it, I was urbane, quick, and secretly wanted a larger canvas. I had hoped a man would bring it to me. That I picked a completely wrong man for that was beside the point. Life would outwit my worst efforts.

I wanted him to teach me how to settle down. In the end, neither of us wanted to be taught anything.

My carpenter decided to take a break from building his house to move to New York. I could not imagine him free in New York and vulnerable to other women who would see his poetic forlornness and treat him so much better than I did, so I begged him to let me come there and be with him. I felt I could not live without him.

In this way, we started to build a life away from our respective pasts. On weekends we often went to his house by the sea. I would put my feet on the dashboard and read to him from novels as we sat in Connecticut traffic. In New York, I studied writing and introduced him to all my friends. He worked at renovating storefronts for businesses all over New York. I wrote ad copy.

We spent weekends away. In Maine. The Rio Grande. Key West. New Jersey shore. Santa Fe. Rome. London. This we did with his carpentry earnings.

I took him to the Philharmonic on my earnings.

He listened to my fictional stories.

I listened to his annoyance with the New York police, with how the union stole his tools, how difficult the business of a one man building business in a city as tough as this was.

We argued constantly but were indelibly committed to each other's weaknesses. I flirted with other men but loved only him.

I kept wanting to leave him but I couldn't. There was only one solution to the way we were ill suited: get married.

My mother's lover, being married and across the ocean, was what is now called "unavailable." So was the man I married in how we could not reach across our ocean, even though we tried, our ocean of incompatibility.

❋ Thirteen

At fifteen, I lived in the movies. In the movies, people were not timid like me, men fought for women, and women fought for love. In the movies, obstacles were overcome. In the movies, a mother eventually found out that her daughter was someone everyone admired. In the movies, people took a chance on love.

So if I wasn't at school, in a bar by myself, or with my father, you could safely assume I was at the movies. French movies where women had pouty mouths and short skirts and were always jealous of some other woman. French movies where men willingly made fools out of themselves only to eventually lie on a bed and have a woman explain the whole mess to him in her black lace underwear. Where everything led to bed.

I was coming out of one of these films, considering going to a second. It was American which everyone knew was inferior, all that action those capitalists insisted on when anyone with any artistic sense knew the real action was in a close-up. I was debating with myself and wondering whether to go down to Mountain Street instead and star in my own movie, when I heard, "What are you doing here?"

Jim Lawrence. The scarf, the knowing smile.

I was sure I was going to see whom he really went out with now. I was curious what his true love was like because surely it couldn't be that Viennese faux woman I was related to.

"I'm alone. How was the movie?" he asked. "I'm about to go in."

He went to the movies alone? A man who was on television.

I gave him some serious movie review, I am sure.

He stared at me. No doubt I was tossing my hair a la Bardot or looking above it all like Jeanne Moreau. I may even have been feigning a slight accent as I gave my report.

"Are you going to the next movie?" I asked. "What ees eet?"

"Steve McQueen," he said, "I love him."

I shrugged.

"Why don't you join me?"

I hesitated. I didn't really like the sound of the American movie. But I did like the sound of someone inviting me. "Sure," I said.

I jumped over to his line, found my stub in my dirtying yellow coat which I was holding since the buildings in Montreal are overheated nine months of the year as compensation for the outdoors. My t-shirt buttons were artfully open, to show off my breasts. My bell sleeves were longer than my arms but showed off my long hands.

Lizard hands, a man in a bar once said, for their thin length. This annoyed me but remained one of those remarks I cannot forget.

"Do you want some popcorn?" he asked.

"Okay," I said and he got us two bags.

We put our legs up on the back of the seats in front of us and sank down deep into our velvet cocoons. This was a happy turn of events to find someone, on this lonely afternoon, to play with.

"How come you're not with what's-her-name?" I asked.

He laughed. "I'm not with her all the time, you know."

Who could be, I thought.

It felt good to be with a man who was in a way related to me. He wasn't someone I had picked up. He wasn't a drunk like my father who never went to the movies. "Waste of time," he said, as if he were J. Paul Getty building an empire.

I sat there and when a particularly interesting shot or witty piece of dialogue came on, I looked over at Jim to make sure he noted it. He laughed. I finally realized the joke was on me, and then I began parodying myself. He seemed to be having quite a good time.

And I was having a good time being a fifteen-year-old girl with a sexy man who might want to make a pass at me but most likely wouldn't. That meant I could actually flirt a little harder. There were no consequences if I really turned on the sex appeal. So I did some provocative pouting during the movie and slunk in my chair so that my breasts sort of popped up. I didn't wear a bra, thinking that it showed I was a free spirit.

After the movie, we put on our coats and scarves and felt that drain one has after having been ridden through another world, that drain of caring for fictional characters whom we now would forget, that intense drain that most of the time we don't offer real people in our own lives.

"Want to go have a drink?" I asked.

He looked at his watch. "Where?" he asked.

"Well we could go to La Coupole or Le Bistro or the Ritz bar. There's even a bar close by here in Place Vendome."

"You know a lot of places."

"Yes," I said proudly.

"Come on, then show me your favorite."

We trudged over wet gray snow past a small French restaurant where a woman in a fur coat and a man in a dark coat with a maroon cravat stood in the doorway arguing about how to get their car out from between two snow banks, and we passed a small place that indicated with a line drawing of a naked woman that there were girls girls girls in there. I immediately compared myself to the line drawing, not favorably, then we strolled past L'eglise St Jude, a small Gothic Catholic church. Suddenly we arrived at La Coupole, which turned out to be warm and pink. There were red tablecloths on the tables and the young waiter strode over and smiled at me, recognizing me no doubt from the last movie excursion I had been on, although I would have been in La Coupole alone.

"I'll have a cognac," I said.

"The same," Jim said.

The waiter looked quizzically at me. He was about 21, probably a French student, with quick black eyes and the insolent air of someone who might quit his job any minute. He studied us for a minute as if to intrude in our meeting and then went off.

"You're an amazing girl," Jim said.

"Why?" I asked.

"You seem to take a lot of matters into your own hands."

"I don't have much choice," I said maturely.

"No you probably don't," he said, "but your mother's not all that bad."

"I don't blame her completely. My father's kind of crazy too."

The waiter brought our drinks. "Anyt'ing else?"

I wanted to say "Two eggs side by each" because I thought that

French Canadianism so funny but I knew this waiter wouldn't find it funny, he was serious about being French Canadian. He was one of those people probably studying at University of Montreal. He kept staring at me accusingly.

Why didn't I get a meaningful political life, his black eyes shot out, instead of being a silly girl with English speaking old men? Finally he went to the bar and lurked there, and began talking to one of the waitresses who was older than him.

"You drank your drink kind of fast," Jim said, looking at my empty glass returning to the table.

"I know, I do everything fast. I even finish my exams first at school. My handwriting is fast, or the way I think."

I should have asked him something about himself then, knowing that you're supposed to talk about men to get their interest but I thought Let's Stay on Me for a Change.

Then he said, "What do you dream about being when you grow up?"

I was too sophisticated to admit that I dreamed of being famous, a film star, especially since I had never acted a day in my life. My plan was to be discovered for the latent talent that was so obviously in me. "I think I'll be a writer."

"You like to write?"

"I write the school plays. I'm usually one of the best in composition. I'm always hugely embarrassed when I have to read in front of the study hall, but I always get picked."

"Why?"

"I write what I see."

He nodded. "When you see it."

"True."

"What do you want to write?"

"Movies, I guess."

"Has anybody talked to you about studying?"

"You mean college?"

"Yes."

"Oh I don't think I can go. My father has no money. And my mother—you know, well you know about her. . . . She doesn't care what I do. And also," I rushed in, "colleges are pretty bourgeois. I think I'll learn from life. My father says you learn nothing in college anyway."

"That's not exactly true."

"Well, his being broke is."

"You could get a scholarship. You're bright."

"I could," I said, "but I don't think I'd fit in."

"In class?"

"I get very embarrassed."

"You wouldn't feel safe," he said.

This was an odd connection to me. I was a bit startled. It's true, I didn't feel safe but it was the first time I had actually considered it. My goal was to weather those feelings of not fitting in, to weather not having any safety. One day I might come out into a sunny safe plateau. I had to.

"But you seem to have no fear going about the city alone," he continued. "You're not embarrassed here for instance."

"No," I said confused. "I get embarrassed when people want to know me."

"Ah . . . " he replied and sat back on the banquette. "What is going to become of you," he said to himself.

"Oh," I said. "I'll persevere."

He smiled. "You will. Do you drink like this all the time?" he asked.

"Oh yes," I said proudly. "Everyone does in my family. Except her."

"But why do you drink?"

"I don't know. It gives me warmth."

"You should get a boyfriend for that."

"I don't like boys," I said, looking over at the waiter, who was still talking to the waitress.

"What do you like?"

"Men," I said.

This was a lie. I was frightened of men, boys, girls, even myself.

"Well," he stood up. He wrapped his scarf round his neck. He looked down at me rather softly, as if I was fragile which clearly was an enormous misinterpretation on his part. "I should get going. I'll see you. This was fun."

"It was."

"Are you just going to stay here?" he asked.

"I think so. I don't mind," I said, pointing to my *Portnoy's Complaint*. "I'll read."

"The light's not good enough."

"I'll still read."

I smiled up at him, having transformed my act from ingénue to Charlie Chaplin waif.

"Okay then." He paid for the drinks and patted my head and gave me a kiss on the cheek and waved cheerily as he left the bar.

The waiter turned to watch him go. He looked over at me as if trying to understand why we weren't leaving together and then he seemed to give up. I opened my book, but I didn't really read anything. I too, was trying to understand why I always ended up sitting alone.

✳ Fourteen

I did spend some time with my mother in those days.

I'd go over in the afternoon, after having had a cognac and sandwich at Le Bistro and, slightly tipsy and inflated on images of my inevitable glamorous future, I would flail down on her couch. She'd just be getting up and making herself an instant coffee. I was disappointed because a truly glamorous person would make cappuccino.

I, however, got everything to go which was evidence of my own brand of glamour. I was of the world outside.

I always brought a coffee up with me to her apartment and added scotch to it when she wasn't looking. Not that she ever said anything about the scotch, but I did not like revealing my intimacy with alcohol.

If she'd been paying attention, it would have been obvious, as it had been to Jim Lawrence. She would have wondered why I passed out at night, from my patrolling of bars or sitting mute and patient in her apartment, sipping for hours. She'd have noticed that I always finished the bottle of wine she brought out, and that I then opened a second one and finished that with such stealth that she thought it was the first one to begin with.

But she didn't notice. And I kept drinking, always with a vengeance at her apartment. My father had schooled me that there was nothing worse than a drunk woman, or rather a woman who showed she was drunk, so somehow, I would drink, get provocative and voluble, when asked, on whatever subject I was talking or fantasizing about, and then quickly pass out when it would be that time for unsteady walking or jagged tears.

There would be those occasional Saturday afternoons when the sun hid coquettishly behind clouds, not quite ready to give us Spring, and I would arrive after one of my cognac lunches, flushed and obviously ready for anything, except closeness, and she would say, "I'm going out tonight, and I need to buy some stockings. I'm going to walk across to the Alexis Nihon Plaza."

One of the many things I did not like about my mother was she was not profligate with money. She hated to spend it and when speaking of money she always sounded angry. I especially did not like it because my father made out she had lots of money.

"How about going to Holt Renfrew?" I asked. Holt Renfrew being on more elegant Sherbrooke, with its sculptures and well-dressed shoppers, near the Ritz Carlton hotel.

I didn't like the fact my mother went to all these outlet places. I never lowered myself to mix with the riff raff this way. I would opt to owe my father or anyone else money rather than buy common stockings in common drugstores.

"That's ridiculous for stockings," she said. "You need to be more practical."

Only boors were practical, in my mind, so I dismissed that piece of advice as part of her miserliness in love. How could a person be worthy of real love in cheap stockings?

However, I wanted her to like me. "Okay I'll go with you."

She put on one of her fur coats that seemed to swamp her small body. Already I felt I towered over her, when in reality it was just my inner unsteadiness that towered.

We crossed the street to the Place Alexis Nihon and I put my nose in the air at this Pharmacie, a place my father would never go into, I decided, as if this Pharmacie was in competition with his bars.

"Want to go out for a snack?" I asked.

"I'm not hungry darling."

"Oh."

She bought some nylons and pulled her red wallet from her handbag and paid carefully with the colored Canadian dollars. She put the change just as carefully back in her change purse.

We left the Pharmacie, now headed for the shopping mall exit. I busied myself looking in the cheap store windows. White vinyl coats. Fake leather shoes with huge platform heels. Photo kiosks. Imitation

American hot dog stands. Throngs of "pepsis" which they called the teenaged French Canadians and I never knew why (did they like Pepsi? Don't Americans?) smoking cigarettes in fake black leather jackets. Tiny tight mini-skirts over leggings. Hoop earrings. Black eyeliner. Vente. Vente. Vente.

We were now outside and she was bending against the cold wind as we made our way up Atwater.

"Where are you off to tonight?" she asked.

"Oh I don't know. I think I'll roam about."

We waited for the light to change. She was officious about this, as if teaching me. I never waited and prided myself on all my near misses of being hit by traffic. I believed I would die being hit by a car. This was my inevitable fate. I was waiting, with all the powerful feelings of self-doom that accompany a life fueled by alcohol.

We stood at the corner as she studied the light. I felt like a racehorse at the gate, ready to bolt. Her mouth was somewhat bitterly smiling to itself, as if she knew she was torturing me.

"I like roaming," I said. "I meet people."

"I suppose."

The light changed.

In a moment, the doorman in her building opened the door. "Bonjour Madame de Bellefeuille."

"Bonjour," she said. Obviously, she could be pleasant to some people.

We waited for the elevator.

"It's funny," she said. "It's harder to meet men as you get older."

I said, "I meet too many men."

"Well you're lucky."

"You have Jim. You had Etienne."

"Yes, but it's so much fun to meet new ones," she said. "Anyway I like Jim but it won't go anywhere. He doesn't want to get married. Etienne was awful to live with. No sense of humour."

The elevator door opened and she looked distastefully at two messy families exiting in disarray. She pulled her fur coat tighter round her body.

I was surprised she wanted to get married.

"I wish men didn't always want to be lovers," I said.

She laughed as we were going up.

"Funny how life is," she said.

"I could introduce you," I said. "I meet men all the time in bars. Some of them aren't bad."

"Really?" she asked, girlishly. We were now going down her hall to her apartment. I hated the hall carpet that had orange in it. I didn't trust the color orange. But when I thought about it, it was because she actually wore that garish a color. More proof of her shortcomings.

"Jackie?" we heard from the other end of her floor.

I turned. It was the Jamaican woman I had met while waiting for an elevator. She was a guardian to a woman in one of the apartments who lay on a stretcher all the time with polio. I had smiled at the invalid woman under her crocheted blankets and she at me, once when she was waiting for an elevator, and the woman on the stretcher told me she was a painter. She invited me into her apartment to see her watercolors of flowers. Huge abundances of blue Irises. She painted with her mouth.

"Jackie, nice to see you," the guardian said.

"Yes. How is Annie?"

"She'd be delighted if you dropped by."

"This is my mother," I said. My mother nodded to the guardian, embarrassed. "I'll drop by later."

"Good. Annie will like it."

The guardian disappeared, having dropped her newspapers off at the incinerator.

My mother unlocked the apartment door, threw her keys down in the dish on the mahogany table in the hallway, took off her coat and hung it up while asking, "Who is that?"

"She takes care of a woman on your floor who has polio. She's an artist," I said proudly, evilly. Like you are not. She has soul. "She paints with her mouth because her arms and legs are frozen. The paintings are quite lovely. She's a nice woman."

"You make the oddest friends," my mother said.

I threw my coat down.

"Hang it up," she said.

I did awkwardly.

"What do you mean?"

"Just remember," my mother said, "nice people don't get anywhere."

I didn't care. I was going to stay with the "nice" crowd anyway.

"Do you want a Dubonnet?" I asked.

"Okay," she said.

I poured her a Dubonnet and me a scotch. Neither of us had any.

She lay down on the couch. Boldly, I sat next to her reclining body. She looked at me oddly.

I was mesmerized by the contours of her body. That she had a waist, a long elegant neck, as if these were accomplishments. I was rounder, messier, my hair fell everywhere, my hips were wider. I felt in constant disarray. In other words, I felt my insides were visible on the outside.

"So as I said," I continued, "I could fix you up."

She said, "Alright, go ahead." She looked at me and put her creamed hand lightly on me. "You really are a sweet girl, aren't you?"

I smiled awkwardly. "Well I don't know about sweet."

"Well you're intelligent," she said.

"I think so."

"You must take after me. Gerald is not intelligent."

"I agree," I said.

"He has class," she said.

"I guess."

"No he does. That was what attracted me. He has real class. You don't see it often."

"But he's not smart," I said.

"No he isn't."

"Jim Lawrence is."

"Yes. I think so," she said.

"Sydney is."

"Very," she said. "I like intelligent men. Sex is in the brain. And other places but they have to interest you. That's why the game part is such fun. It's a battle of wits. Why don't you have a boyfriend?" she asked.

"Sometimes I like someone but often it doesn't work out."

"Maybe you don't give it a chance. You seem to roam around a lot."

I didn't know what she meant. The roaming seemed to me the essence of life. A man was supposed to know how to stop me, not me stop for a man. This was a subtlety I expected everyone to understand.

"I don't think you've ever loved anyone," she said.

"Maybe not."

"You have to take a risk," she said. "You can't be timid. I think you're timid."

I looked away. How could I, the patroller of bars and men's eyes, be timid? Clearly she didn't see who I really was.

"I'll take a risk with someone worth it," I said.

"Yes, you're young. Perhaps you will. I wish I was young."

"Everyone wants to be young. I don't know why."

"Your life is in front of you."

"Well what's wrong with living it now?" I asked.

"Nothing," she said, "nothing at all. It's just that it takes you a long time to know how to live it. If at all."

"Do you know how to?"

"Yes. I think so. I work, it's important to work. To not be dependent. All men leave, you know that. And then it's important to risk loving. It's the only thing that matters."

It seemed to me she was leaving out the gray areas. Everyone, my father included, had these platitudes, these pronouncements about life, but nobody talked about how to cope with the fears in living, the gray things, like how you could love someone and not like them, or you wanted to love someone but couldn't or you were good at something but that wasn't what you wanted to be good at. Nobody talked about the ambiguities.

I resented that and sipped my drink.

"You are a sweet girl," she said.

Nobody talked about the real issues.

✳ Fifteen

Studies came easily to me, which is to say I spent my time at my desk writing notes to myself. As soon as classes were over, I avoided school-planned recreation activities and slipped into the music rooms where I would improvise haunting, haunted pieces at the piano. I would play, looking out the windows of the small wooden piano cubicles at the quiet afternoon city streets, as if I were Beethoven himself. I felt safe in those rooms, nurtured by my gentle interaction with the notes.

Either I played the piano or I was playing records in my room upstairs. I wasn't interested in playing sports with the other girls and even though I was benign and friendly, it was as if I were years older.

The girls told me their problems and I nodded my head, wisely, and gave sage advice, pretending I was my father at the bar.

But most of the time, I roamed the school, alone, dreaming. I didn't long for drink. I replaced the release drink gave me with the piano, with listening to music. I replaced it with fantasies, sitting at my desk, of how reckless and free my life was going to be.

I don't remember a serious crush at that time. Perhaps there were boys I met or men in the bars whom I would call from the school's wooden payphone boxes, but I had no great passion that I recall. I was more like a prisoner calling to the outside world. I liked to know I had contact.

I didn't call my father often because he was hard to reach and, if I did get him, he wasn't sure what to do with a conversation. I didn't call my mother. Sometimes she called me to tell me she was going away for the weekend so please do not use her apartment since she worried about me being careless and burning things with my cigarettes. Or I would call her to ask her if I could use her apartment, would she be away, and sometimes she said yes and sometimes she said no, as if she had forgotten her fear of my burning down her apartment. Her moods fluctuated, I believed, with the vicissitudes of her love life.

She never visited me at school but my father did. I'd be called out of study hall and told I had a visitor, and, there in the large room that looked like a sitting room with flower-covered couches and bare dark wood tables would be my tall, unsteady father alone, saying "Hello Darling."

"Anything wrong?" I asked.

"I was just at the hospital across the street. My heart. They're doing more tests."

I felt a pang in my own heart. What if he was seriously ill?

He had often woken me Monday mornings to take me to school and told me he had just had a heart attack. "I'm alright," he would say. "I took the pills." I would walk bleary eyed and frightened down the stairs and he'd say, "I'm past it you know."

On the way to school I would sit in the car crying.

"What are you crying about?" he asked.

"Your heart."

"Oh I'll be alright."

He was only 57, he said, but his heart was bad and I would visit him in the hospitals after some of these heartquakes and we'd play Whisk and he'd explain angina to me. He frequently had gout too, a gentleman's disease he said, in other words to be expected. I was frightened at the thought of losing him, but vaguely curious to see if I could weather that too. As I was to learn later, the only limit of pain is greater pain.

But at that time, it seemed he put me in the frame of mind of losing. I didn't want him to die, and thought that might be protection enough, but seeing him there, just back from the doctor, frightened me. Had he come to tell me something horrible?

"Are you alright Daddy?"

"I'll go on a few more years."

"I want you to tell me the truth."

"I am."

"Then why are you here?"

"I came to see my old pal."

"Why don't you take me out of here? You can get permission."

"No I can't. I'm frightened of the nuns."

"I thought you want to sleep with them."

"You can want to sleep with someone and be frightened at the same time."

How many fathers, I wondered, admitted to wanting to sleep with the nuns? I put my arms around him, "Daddy, I love you." I was shocked suddenly that I was the size of a grown woman. I wasn't going to his waist anymore. I pulled away, embarrassed.

"I know. I love you too."

"Alright then why are you here?"

"Jesus, you're suspicious."

"You can't say Jesus like that here," I said teasingly.

"Oh sorry."

"You can't ask the nuns out for dinner either. Or where they get their outfits because I don't want to wear one of those habits, thank you. Not the wimple anyway."

He laughed.

He sat down in his coat. "God I get so tired," he said.

"Of what?"

"Oh they want to cut my commissions selling the damn bridge grating because they think I'm making too much money. The idiots."

"That's not fair."

"No it isn't. I'm tired of travelling. I like it on one hand—the time alone but one's always pushing, driving. One step ahead of one's debts."

"I know."

"You do, do you?" he said.

"Well I'm in debt all the time too."

"I know," he said.

"I'll pay you back when I'm older."

"Have you spoken to Lisbeth?"

"No."

We were silent.

"Did you see her on TV?" I asked. I liked this part of her life. On television she couldn't hurt me.

"No. I don't watch that rubbish," he replied.

I looked over at my big sad father, who seemed to sisyphus-like be working his way through life, to take care of me and his drinks. He wanted to believe in life being good and love lasting but he didn't really believe it so instead he accorded himself the illusory pleasure of drink, not that I understood all that then, but looking at him, I felt it.

I felt his terrible need of illusion. And looking at him, I felt I would be in terrible need of it too. We just weren't doing that well at going off into a stellar life. We seemed to be carrying some failure around with us, which at different times, we gave the name Lisbeth.

If I needed money and he was not available, my mother was to blame. If he couldn't make my school payments without terrific juggling and bouncing of checks, it was my mother who should be contributing something goddamit. Why can't she do anything?

This is the role we gave her.

I looked at his sadness and put my hand on his arm and said, "We'll be together Friday night. We can have dinner and talk about things."

"Yes," he said. "Well you probably have people to play with and so on."

"I'm too old to play, Daddy."

"You should study probably."

"Yeah."

I wanted him to leave because I couldn't make him feel better and, at the same time, I wanted him to stay so I could find a way to make him happy.

"Want to lie down in my room?" I asked. "Take a nap."

"Oh yes", he laughed, "very restful around a bunch of roped-in teen-age girls. I can imagine the quiet."

I held him tighter as I walked him to the big convent doors and kissed him goodbye and said "Thank you for coming" and "Do you have $5?" which he did and I kissed him again, accomplices in need, and I watched him leave the convent and take his big weight down the stairs on slippery men's shoes and open his car door as if it weighed a lot too. I watched him speed out of there.

I turned sharply back into the inner school and looked at the time, time for dinner, one eats early in boarding schools, and as I hurried down the steps to the refectory hall, I became furious at my mother. Couldn't she do anything to make us happy? Why did she get off?

This anger turned slowly into some kind of self-lecture that I had the right to do anything I pleased, and if they were going to play this way, then I would too, that if they didn't want to be normal parents, then fuck it, I didn't have to be normal either, I would be my own person, live my own rules, and I turned around to go back upstairs to the phones because no one would be on them now, everyone was eating downstairs, and I pulled a dime out of my uniform, always ready to buy myself a treat, and I dialed 411 for the number of Jim Lawrence.

I deserved to have a drink with someone who showed some interest in me. Someone who saw that I had potential. He liked me and I began to say things to myself like, "I don't care if he's her boyfriend and she thinks it's odd. Who are we all to begin standing on ceremony?"

And even as I dialed the number I felt more womanish, freer, ready for a sophisticated life.

There was no answer. I'd try later.

"Jackie?"

It was Mother Power. The head nun who had once called me into her office when I was ten and told me I was too nonchalant. I spent the year trying to figure out what she meant. More accurately, I spent my life trying to figure out what she meant, and finally decided it means you're not feeling something when it hurts.

But I had ways of feeling and she knew it.

"I wanted to ask you," she said, "if you know a way to help me solve a problem. Come in," she said, "come in to my office."

Obviously she wasn't going to ask me why I wasn't at supper. Still, I said, "My father just came to visit me."

"Ah," she said, sitting down plumply at her roll up desk, "your father."

We both said nothing, understanding the burdens of men.

"Do you know Marilyn Hill?"

"No."

"She's younger than you and has just started here. She's from Winnipeg. She has cerebral palsy."

I nodded.

Mother Power waited.

"What's that?" I asked.

"It's a disease that affects her speech, her motor system. It affects her movements. She moves awkwardly, she shuffles, lopsided; it's very difficult for her. She sounds like she's talking through a bubble when she speaks. Sometimes she can't get out what she wants to say. She's had many operations but. . . She has done well, though. She can write out her own schoolwork, which many people can't. Even those who don't have cerebral palsy."

I inhaled my breath. How can this Marilyn person live?

"She's a wonderful girl," Mother Power continued. "Bright, a sense of humor. But who will room with her? Obviously it would take special patience. What do you recommend I do?"

"Well I can of course," I said.

She narrowed her sharp dark eyes behind her John Lennon glasses. "Oh really. Why would you want to do that?" she asked.

"Well . . . well . . . I want to help. It doesn't bother me."

Mother Power stood up. "I thought you might say that. You're kind, Jacqueline. Very kind."

This was as strange a description to me as "nonchalant." Where did she come up with these for me? How come she didn't say "brilliant" or "attractive"?

"Girls can be very silly," Mother Power said. "They can make fun of people not as advantaged as themselves. That's something I imagine you don't do."

I wasn't following her. My mind was already on being kind to Marilyn Hill. I would encourage her. I would learn her particular brand of humor. I would rally her on. I would salve the loneliness she feels. I wouldn't let her feel disadvantaged.

I came back to Mother Power's voice. "I'll have both your things moved into a room and then tonight you can become friends as you set things up."

"Okay."

I started to leave because I remembered I wanted to call Jim Lawrence. He wouldn't use kind. He might use brilliant or beautiful. The right words.

"I have to make a phone call," I said.

Mother Power was looking at something. "Don't lose it," she said.

"What?"

"Your vivacity."

I smiled and moved out of there quickly. I didn't want her inadvertently insulting me anymore.

✳ Sixteen

Marilyn, without cerebral palsy, would have been considered pretty. She had long brown blonde hair and freckles and even features, a Cheryl Tiegs understudy. But she also had one arm that was clawed into itself, her posture was crooked, and she opened her mouth cavernously to speak in her hoarse foghorn voice. Her uniform was longer on one side than the other, due to her misshapenness.

However, Marilyn's eyes danced and we instantly took to each other (I admired her lack of self pity. Why was it the people who had everything were the ones who whined all the time?). And I immediately recognized her sly humour even if I didn't understand what she was saying. I understood that she was teasing. I thought it nothing less than heroic.

I helped her make her bed and put her things in the oak drawers we each had. I hung up her uniforms and her normal clothes for weekends. I put out her family photos, a nice-looking father who looked young enough to be my father's son, a mother with Marilyn's face without the illness. She loved her parents, she told me. Did I have any pictures?

"No," I said, "my parents are . . . picturesque. I'll tell you about them another time."

I had no pictures and no knickknacks from my father's bar homes, but I did have my record player. This is my family album, I explained. My piece de resistance. I played Camelot for her as we undressed and told her that I always got tears in my eyes when Lancelot saves Guinevere.

Marilyn, I saw, was not so emotional, and I realized at that moment, that infirmity and all, Marilyn might do better in life than I. She was not a wreck inside. Just on the outside.

But I would pretend, for her benefit, that I was not a wreck. That I was strong and capable and loving.

As we lay in bed, waiting for lights out, I asked her when she got the cerebral palsy. As a small child. "You can live with it," she said.

I told her about the woman who painted with polio. How it made so much sense to me. How everybody was so brave when you thought about it. "How you are," I said. "Coming to this school. Who's your teacher?"

"Mrs. Mrs. Mrs. Mrs. Mcmanus," she finally got out.

"Oh she's good," I said. "A secular who is sexually repressed like the nuns. But she likes to laugh. You'll get on well with her."

I realized Marilyn might never have boys interested in her. I didn't ask about boys, which is what girls do when they first share a room. Do you have a boyfriend? Question number one. I skipped it.

She asked me though.

"Well, not really," I said. I didn't want to talk about me. It might confuse my Joan of Arc image. At least not tonight.

Mother Manley broke into our room. Was it because Camelot was on the record player? "How to handle a woman, ask me well, I will tell you Sir, the way to handle a woman is to love her, simply love her, love her, love her."

Mother Manley of the gray eyebrows and gray skin and dry lips who was shorter than Marilyn and myself. "There is a phone call for you, Jacqueline."

Usually phone calls weren't good news. I had just seen my father. So who could this be? I wrapped my dressing gown around my nightgown and put on Marilyn's slippers and followed Mother Manley's silent swishing habit down the cavernous hallway, down the dark stairway, to the entry area of the Convent where the incoming phone box hung in the dark. I went in. She switched on the light from the outside.

"Hello?"

"Yes."

"Daddy."

"Yes."

"I just saw you."

"Yes."

"What's wrong?"

"Nothing."

"Where are you?"

"At the Cavalier."

"What are you doing?"

"What do you think I'm doing?"

"Well why are you calling?"

"I was thinking about you."

I couldn't hear a slur in his words. His slurs were not caused by ce-rebral palsy, a subject I was now an expert on.

"What are you thinking?" I asked.

I found myself looking forward to his answer because I loved lis-tening to his British voice. My father had the voice of a British actor, Jack Hawkins. It was my father's voice and the way he snapped the ciga-rette lighter shut when he lit a woman's cigarette that made me think he could handle things, he would come through.

"What did you say Daddy?"

"I said, I was thinking how you used to be a little girl and now you, you seem so grown up."

This was delightful news.

"What do I look like?"

"Well, you look. . . . " he didn't know what to say.

"Good?" I asked teasing.

"No," he suddenly sobered up, "you look alright."

"Daddy. Guess what? I got a new roommate named Marilyn."

"Is she as crazy as you are?"

"She will be," I said.

"No doubt."

"Say hello to everyone at the bar. Are you lonely? Is that it?" I asked.

"Everyone's lonely."

"You think so?"

"Yes."

"What's the cure?"

"Drink."

"No really."

"For me it's drink."

"For me," I said, "it's dreams."

"Well that's nice," he said.

"It is."

"Alright, I'll pick you up Friday."

"No, I forgot, I'm going to stay at Lisbeth's."

"I thought you said she's away."

"That's why. Maybe we can meet for lunch."

"Alright. We'll do that."

"I'll call you."

I switched off the light of the phone box and then I went back up the quiet hallways, I went back up the stairs to my room.

But when I got there, Marilyn was asleep. Perhaps the exhaustion of a new school, new room.

I turned to my record player, which I couldn't turn on at this hour. But, I realized, it wasn't Camelot I wanted to hear anyway. I was no Guinevere. My father was no King

Arthur or Lancelot.

I lay down and thought how my father was probably very different than Marilyn's father, Mr. Hill. I thought of my father's long fingers. How they circled a drink, how they grasped my shoulder. I thought about how he said women were awful, how he said I would have no one but him. I thought about how some days he thought everything was possible for us and on other days we might not make it till five o'clock.

I thought of how kind he was to barmaids and to people he met in passing. How he liked to talk about the weather and the economy to people he happened to be sitting next to. How he was willing to say anything to them but not willing to have a conversation with me that would explain how I was going to live my life.

It meant I had to do it on my own.

"You'll find out," he would say, "you'll find out how difficult it is not to make a mess of your life."

I thought he was wrong.

I would not make a mess of my life. That's what I told myself as I rubbed my hands on his tweed jacket for the solidity of his back inside it, hoping the tweed jacket's pedigree would rub off on me. I stroked it and was proud of my father's arrogance for not buying a new jacket just because he had a cigarette burn on the cuff of this comfy old one. I would straighten his tie as he was sitting facing the bar. I would touch his hair.

"What are you doing?" he'd jerk away.

"Let's talk about sex," I'd say.

"Get your hands off me. Find someone younger."

"I would never go for anyone as crazy as you anyway," I'd say to the bar mirror.

"And I wouldn't want anyone like you either," he laughed. "I'm no fool."

* Seventeen

That Saturday night it seemed the Bistro was quieter than usual. Even, my friend, the older woman was not there. Perhaps she was with her boyfriend. I tried calling my father on the bar's pay phone in the back of the bistro near the ladies room. I tried a journalist who covered Quebec City whom I had met at the bar. I tried my father, I tried the journalist. No one answered. I called information and got the number of Jim Lawrence again. He answered.

"This is Jacqueline. Lisbeth's daughter. You know. With dark hair."

"Of course I know who you are. How are you?"

"I was wondering if you'd like to um, come down to um, the Bistro on Mountain and um, join me for a drink. I'll buy," I said quickly. "If you don't have time or you can't, I completely understand—"

"You're there now?"

"Yes."

He hesitated. "It'll take me about 15 minutes."

"Okay."

I went to the ladies room and freshened my lipstick. I plumped up my hair and felt rather annoyed that I looked sort of young when it was my intention to look worn and world-weary. I went back to the wooden table and sat down to wait. I thought: I have just called my mother's lover.

It wasn't my fault that I liked him as a person.

Jim walked rather uneasily into the Bistro. He wasn't a barfly like myself or my father, and he walked in rather gingerly, his eyes scanning the room nervously. Still he seemed bigger than all the craning men at the bar, he seemed full, as if he had a life and was not one of those standing up there looking for one.

He saw me and smiled and then came to my table. Instantly I was nervous.

"Hi," he said.

Suddenly I got all coy. I smiled nervously. "I don't know why I asked you but—"

"It's okay. I'm glad you did."

The waiter came and he ordered a beer. It was distressing to me to notice that in some way Jim looked out of place here. He looked like he did other things. Everybody else in the bar seemed to be lingering, while he looked as if he went to and from places.

"So what have you been doing?" he asked.

"I was in school. I took my exams."

"How'd you do?"

"Well. Actually, I came in first in the province in Latin."

"You're kidding? Why didn't you tell anyone? That's amazing."

"I don't know—" I said. I suddenly felt like I was boasting, even though it was the truth. But why was I mentioning it?

"I came in third in composition."

"Third what?" Jim asked.

"Third in the province."

"Jacqueline, not everyone does that. That's fantastic. But when do you study? You're always out and about."

"No, I study." I said. "At school, in the afternoons. And the weekend before my exams, I went to Quebec City with a journalist I met here and just studied."

"Just studied?"

"Yes," I said, which was true. There was something in me that wanted to do well.

"Oddly, I believe you," he said. "Anyway this is marvelous about how you aced those tests."

Now I almost felt sick at this bald attention. It was as if I were under too intense a spotlight.

"But I was bad in math."

"Well so what?" he said, and now that I had confirmed I was bad in something, things felt more as they should be. I began to warm up again to the low lighting, and rub my fingers around the cognac rim, and return to my natural pose of posing in a bar, and I leaned forward and put my face up to the light and started smiling because, let's face it, it was nice to have someone be interested in me, particularly in my exams which everyone looked down at as the plaything of a child, so no one had really asked, my father and mother and their friends being far more interested in the burgeoning sexuality I was half-flaunting and half-staving off, so I found myself girlishly smiling because Jim Lawrence seemed to know there were other parts to me. I thought I'd return to the subject of my exams, since therein seemed to lay unusual success for me. "I always finish so fast that I think I didn't do well. Or that I forgot a page or something."

"You told me that."

"What do you think that is?"

"Either you're very smart, which is something that has crossed my mind, or you're very anxious, which has crossed my mind too."

I began moving my fingers, strangely.

It was snowing outside. I could see from my table through the glass windows and doors.

Anxious. I hadn't thought of that.

"What about college?" he asked again. "Aren't the nuns pushing you?"

It's true. They had been bringing it up. But I just couldn't get my father to fill out the paperwork with me and then his lack of interest would depress or anger me and then I'd say, "Oh never mind, I don't want to go anyway."

My mother did not seem to know that I should be going to college. Or maybe because she had not gone, she felt I didn't need to. My mother didn't seem to know, never had known, that I needed help of any kind.

Anyway, I told myself, I want to live. I just want to live. Not knowing that that statement alone gave away how much I felt I was dying inside.

Fueled by my insistence that I wanted to live, I quickly switched the conversation to him. And he responded kindly, as if knowing that focusing on his life, instead of mine, might be soothing for me.

He told me about anchoring in Toronto. He told me that he was too young to get married; after all he was only thirty-six. He told me that he wouldn't move on to the States, most likely he would write books eventually, non fiction about Canadian politics. Television was a stupid lark. But you got a lot of benefits. People treated you like you were Mahatma Gandhi himself although all you did was talk in front of a piece of machinery and be willing to make a fool of yourself in front of a larger public than most people do.

He told me that women were abundant; you just had to be nice to them.

He told me that there was something about me, a certain defiance that was almost brave, he said, but he wasn't sure, but there was definitely something haunting about me and then we noticed that four hours had gone by and we had been ordering drinks all along.

He didn't say anything about my mother.

My mother. Why wouldn't anyone tell me why she doesn't love me? Am I that bad?

He said, "Where are you going now?"

I didn't want to say to her house since that would make her spectre present. And I couldn't really stay at his place, so I hesitated and then said, "I'll walk you home."

I decided that after I left him I would go to an after-hours revolutionary club and spend time there.

It was cold out but he lived ten blocks away so he said, "Let's take a taxi."

Mountain Street was full of people leaving bars and bistros. People mulling around, smoking cigarettes. People looked at me when they walked by, and I thought it was because I was attractive, but it could be because I was looking so intently at them.

"If we take a taxi, then I can't walk you home," I said.

"You can walk me up my stairs."

The cab stopped in front of his place and Jim paid. Then I got out with him and said nothing as he unlocked the front door and he held it open and spread out one arm for me to go in before him. I went through first. Then I followed him up the carpeted stairs to his apartment.

He switched on a lamp in his hall. We went inside the living room where he didn't switch on a lamp but went right to the stereo and put on some Herbie Hancock. This was before Herbie Hancock went commercial.

He took off his coat and sat down in his armchair in the dark, with the music playing. I sat down on the old couch across from him still in my coat.

"Take your coat off."

I did.

And as we sat silently in the dark, listening to the music, I realized what with the drink and the conversation, I was very tired.

I closed my burning eyes.

It passed through my mind that she wanted me to lose my virginity. But very probably not with him. But what an act of retaliation.

He said, "Do you want to lie down?"

I nodded.

He got up and left the room and I thought he would return with a blanket like so many of the men had at the apartments I found myself ending up in. But instead he came back and handed me his pajamas. "I have only one pair," he said.

"I'll wear the top," I said, "you wear the bottom."

"I said you were intelligent," he replied. "Or you've seen a lot of movies."

He stood there looking at me for a bit and I noticed that his eyes were a little glassy. "Why don't you lie down on my bed? This couch is kind of old," he said.

Which we did. Lie down in his bed.

My mind wasn't sure what to make of anything.

So I let him take control.

I watched as he put his arms around me casually, as if he wasn't really doing it, and I watched myself notice that his arms and chest were naked and strong and I could feel him, as a man. He felt grown up with hair on his chest, and there was so much more of him than me. Yet, because he was wearing pyjama bottoms, he was not threatening.

"Do you think we should kiss?" he asked, smiling.

I really had no desire to kiss him. He was still my mother's boyfriend, belonging to another world.

I said, to be sophisticated, "No. It might get confusing."

"Well," he said dreamily, feigning perhaps drunkenness, "Might be provocative."

"No," I said, while thinking this whole thing of a man's body is so warm and comforting. "We should just sleep. For obvious reasons," I explained soberly. "We should just sleep."

Which was difficult because even though I was covered on top, my legs and bottom were naked, creating a kind of electricity in me, a kind of openness that had to be filled, a kind of wanting to go blank and feel nothing but his legs and himself in and on me, and this electrical charge seemed to get stronger in the bed the more time passed, and our bodies kept heating up what with our sort of politely holding each other every now and then and politely disentangling, while compulsively returning over and over to the soft naked parts of each other.

What was this? I kept asking myself. I had felt "hot" while kissing boys and men but this was a desire to fall into the chasm of a man. I shouldn't be in this bed; I reprimanded myself, yet I couldn't get up. It felt too good lying entwined with a man.

I lay there thinking this, as if thinking would keep me from feeling.

And anyway, I continued, she doesn't care about me so why should I care about her?

We didn't sleep much. About three in the morning, he sat up, and said, "I think we should have sex."

"I can't," I said, "you're my mother's boyfriend."

"Details. . . . " he said.

"We'll feel terrible after."

He snuggled back down with me and put his arms around me. "Oh. So you're here to torture me."

"Yes," I said.

"Alright, smart one," and he held on tight, with an erection, and we snuggled in, in a bond that perhaps was more deepening than if we had done what my mother would have expected us to be doing.

I still didn't sleep. He snored, which made me wonder how women live with that. To distract myself while I lay awake, I congratulated my-self on how different I was from her. I was a rebel. This not having sex with a man she would have sex with. I was different.

Or let me say, it felt that way.

Which is not to say that I didn't call her other boyfriend, Andy, weeks later and go to a double feature in Old Montreal with him. We just watched the movies and talked about them, but it was with him.

Which is not to say that I did not cross and uncross my legs for great attention when Alvin was on the couch with me.

Which is not to say that I was not constantly checking to see how attractive I was, and it seemed like her boyfriends were the men I chose as the litmus tests. I thought the men in the bars would make love with mud, if encouraged, so I was not particularly flattered by their attentions.

But her men, well, if I could distract their eye, then I must be worth something.

✳ Eighteen

Patsy Haber's father was somewhat famous, being a sports commentator. It was he who shouted into the TV microphone during hockey games, "And he scored!" Three words that ran deep in most Montrealers' inner ear, whether they liked hockey or not. There seemed to be a hockey game on somewhere, in some place, all the time. One couldn't avoid it: Hockey players and announcers in one's psyche like family.

"How can you do it?" Patsy asked me.

She was sitting on the school radiator in the hallway, with some of her friends sitting next to her, girls in my class whom I didn't pay much attention to. Her yellow hair was pulled off her face with a black hair band, her pert nose small, set under calculating eyes. Calculating a sturdy, well-kept middle class future.

"Do what?" I asked.

I was still processing having been nominated in front of the entire school for President of the Drama Society, which forced me to stand up and decline because I had never joined the Drama Society. They had nominated me because everyone thought I was a member. True, I did write the school plays but I never joined anything. However, what had occurred to me was that, to my peers, I acted as if I lived in a drama society.

"Room with Marilyn."

Just then Marilyn loped down the corridor where Patsy, her gang and I were sitting in the windowsill ledge near the radiator. Marilyn roared out a "Hi" that came out twisted. She was marvelously brave. I was overcome by it.

The other girls did not respond, embarrassed at her infirmity.

I said, "Where are you going?"

She said to the library but I was the only one who understood that.

"I'll come along," I said and jumped off the sill. I was bored anyway with these girls my own age.

Marilyn looked surprised and gave me a quizzical look. I was hurt by that. Did she think I was weak?

"How's your love life?" I asked.

She laughed. Her notebooks were all scrawled upon.

"Do you like those girls?" she asked. "Is that your upper class clique?"

"Give me a break," I said.

She looked a little hurt and I realized maybe, unlike me, Marilyn wished to be part of that kind of a clique.

"They're just into boys and clothes and their prom," I said. "Not into pornography and existential problems like we are."

She smiled.

She sat down twisted in the library chair, put her stuff on her desk. She was tired.

"What are you looking for here?" I asked.

I didn't know my way round the library since I was too impatient to ever bother to take the time to find something. "Shakespeare's Sonnets."

"Oh. I'll try and find them for you," I said.

She gave me her sly smile. "You won't know how."

"No," I said.

She pointed to the S. "That's a good start," she said.

I nodded and found them and brought them down off a high shelf and gave the book to her.

"Thanks," she said, sweetly.

My head began to hurt. I instantly had a splitting headache. She had said, "Thanks," so trustingly and nakedly. So simply and directly. I was going to cry. It didn't occur to me then how much I was propping myself up on grandiosity, not on the power of humility.

"Yeah you're welcome," I said, confused at this sudden well of feelings.

Friday afternoon, I took my allowance and a taxi across the Mercier Bridge where they said the Indians built the steel girders because they love heights, past the Caughnawaga reservation full of flat one story, one room houses, the yards full of old cars in various forms of disrepair. I was on my way to see my father at the Cavalier Motel Bar.

I walked in and he said, "Oh I forgot to tell you. Lisbeth called for you."

"What about?"

"How should I know? She wants to know when you're graduating."

"This year."

"I know," he said. "Speaking of which, I'm moving."

"What has that got to do with it?"

"To Toronto. I want to write a book. I have a marvelous idea. Do you want me to tell you?"

No, I thought.

"Okay," I said.

Jeanette put a scotch and soda in front of him and a vodka collins in a frosted glass so you couldn't see what was in it in front of me. I smiled complicitly at her.

"This man is hired by the guardian of a beautiful young girl to transport her to an Arab who has paid the guardian to marry her."

I sipped my drink.

"What happens in the end?"

"I'm not sure," he said.

"The guardian no doubt keeps the money," I suggested.

"Probably," he said. "What do you think? It's fantastic, isn't it?"

"It depends how you write it."

"Oh no, you don't know what you're talking about. It's a wonderful story. That's why I want to get away from everyone so I can write it. I'll live in a motel."

"Away from me?"

He didn't look at me. He was talking about leaving as offhandedly as if we were discussing what drink to order. "Oh you'll want to be off doing whatever the hell young people do," he said. "Which is what? What are your plans?"

"Work I suppose. I applied to a college but I haven't heard."

"Who would pay for you to go? That's why I never mentioned going. I haven't got it."

"I know."

"You could ask Lisbeth. She might have it."

"I don't like asking her for things."

He looked at his drink. "I thought you were thick as thieves." He said it slowly, carefully, as if trying to get information.

"I'm not. I just go about the city. I like the city."

"About with whom?"

"Friends."

"What kind?"

"Of hers."

"God help you. They probably all work in television and films."

"You're right."

"Are they nice to you?"

"I like some of them. I like one, this man called Jim Lawrence."

He turned his head to me, cleverer he was than I thought and said, "I thought you said that was her boyfriend."

"I can still like him."

"I suppose." He turned back to his drink. "Why don't you ask her to get you into film? Work in that?"

He turned to me and looked at me strangely.

I went on, "I don't want to be indebted to her."

"Watch out with those people," he said. "She doesn't attract very kind people. Like goes to like you know."

"I know." But I knew he was wrong. Look at him. What could he possibly know about romance and love? Clearly whatever he knew got him nowhere.

I left him and found myself walking up Sherbrooke toward Atwater, and studying the delicate horse sculptures standing next to huge round granite balls as entrance decorations. Why? I wondered. I looked up at the tall elegant stone buildings with their long narrow windows lit by chandeliers behind mysterious white gauze curtains. Who? I wondered.

She opened the door after I knocked.

"Oh. I didn't know you were coming," my mother said, as if she had forgotten a plan. "Do you want a drink?"

"Yes thanks."

I saw a short man with gray hair sitting on her couch. He looked like an old prizefighter. He had glasses on with dark rims, and the glass was tinted. He seemed old.

"Get yourself a Dubonnet," she said.

She went back into the living room and said to the man, "This is my daughter who sort of ambles all over town."

I smiled from the kitchen. He smiled from behind his glasses.

She sat down on her white leather couch next to him, her knit skirt folded pristinely. She put her hand on his chest and sort of quickly rubbed his shirt, as if teasing. He smiled indulgently and purred a bit. I came into the living room and sat across from them and once again noticed the hems of my slacks were down. Why did I only see that at her place? "Don't you have any friends your own age to go out with?" she asked. She lit a cigarette.

Martin, that was his name, said in a deep voice, "I'm glad she came over."

He had not put his hand on her.

"Why can't she find a boyfriend?" she asked him. "What's wrong with you?" she turned back to me. "You're somewhat attractive and everyone says you're bright. Why can't you?"

This hurt my feelings. "Well maybe I do have one."

"Who?" Her dark eyes looked sharply at me.

"I don't want to say."

"Is he married?"

"No but he's somewhat famous," I said.

"You can tell us." She was smiling. I think she believed me.

"I promised I wouldn't."

"Famous how?"

For once, my mind wasn't moving fast.

"You might know him."

She took a drag. "This whole thing sounds bizarre," she said. "I think you're getting crazier and crazier."

"What do you mean?"

"You can't sit still. You laugh at the wrong times, which I think has to do with your smoking marijuana—"

Martin broke in, "She's young. It's their job to be mixed up. Actually, she's quite adorable."

I was confused. Here I was being vilified in front of him by my own mother, and yet he was seeing me as adorable.

"There is something wrong with her," my mother replied.

I wanted to say, "Yes, it's you," but I didn't.

Martin joked, "Do you think there's something wrong with you?"

"You're the editor of the *Montreal Star*?" I asked.

He nodded. "I am."

He smiled at me. "Are you interested in newspapers?"

"I doubt very much she reads one," my mother said. She was looking very annoyed with me.

"Yes, I'm interested. I like parts, I mean. The arts. I read the arts section."

"Lisbeth," he said joking, "How can you have such an adorable daughter who doesn't read the paper?"

I smiled, enjoying being teased, "She pretends I'm deaf and dumb."

My mother looked confused.

I wanted to ask if they were lovers but I kept my mouth shut. Of course they were lovers, everyone was her lover.

I smiled at him desperately, meaning seductively.

"Where's Jim?" I asked her.

"I don't know," she said.

"Jim who?" he asked.

"Jim Lawrence," I replied. "Do you know his work? He writes a column on books for the *Toronto Globe & Mail*."

"I do. He's good."

My mother nodded and cheered up a bit at that.

"What are you good at?" he asked me.

"Running around in circles," my mother responded.

I wanted to say I am good at school but that seemed unsophisticated. I shrugged, instead, showing requisite blaséness.

The phone rang and as my mother went into the bedroom to get it, I furtively undid a button on my t-shirt.

"Where do you do all this roaming about you're so famous for?" he asked me.

"I like the bars on Mountain and Crescent Street."

"Ah. What else do you like to do?"

I looked at him puzzled.

"You know," he said, "like movies, theatre. . . ."

"I like all of that," I said, still confused.

I was at the age where I thought everyone liked all of that.

We were silent. He was very male, it seemed to me, as if he was the first one I'd ever met. It was his steadiness, sitting there. He wasn't jumping about inside. Even my father jumped about inside. I felt stilled by his stillness, the steadiness of his intense hazel eyes (he had taken off his glasses). His eyes were like Picasso's, they were so piercing. It seemed I was a fish he was reeling in. But to where?

My mother returned.

"Martin and I are going to dinner in Old Montreal."

"Ah."

"Martin is one of the few men who can understand my sense of humor," she said.

I thought, that's a feat since you don't have one.

Then he kindly put his arm around her and kissed her on the side of her face, "Yes darling."

What did these men see in her?

Sex. It had to be sex.

I couldn't even see her having sex. She seemed too cold to heat up the way I knew one did. That was all I knew one did.

"Are you still a virgin?" she asked.

"No," I lied.

"Well that's good."

I hated her.

Her phone rang again. She clip clipped into the bedroom at high speed.

Sitting across from Martin, for some reason I didn't even care if it was Jim. Jim now seemed like a nice guy, whereas Martin seemed interestingly complex. I thought there was more intelligence underneath there.

"So," he said, "Your father is British. How does he feel about the French Canadians?"

"He doesn't take the politics seriously."

"They're like that, the Brits. They don't take any culture but their own seriously."

"Well," I said to sound sophisticated, "they're good at theatre."

"You like British theatre?"

I had never thought about it. I sat there feeling non-plussed.

"Why don't you come with me to a Shaw play? I have tickets—you know, the paper. . . ."

"When?"

"On Wednesday."

"I can't," I said. He was asking me out. Just like that. "I have to be in school. Maybe another time," I said boldly.

"Really? I'll call you at your school."

I was shocked. The editor of the *Montreal Star* was going to call me? She returned to the living room.

"Martin, we should go. That was the Spaldings. They're meeting us there."

Martin stood up and I stood up and he shook hands with me and also moved some of the strands of my hair forward from behind my shoulder.

"Adorable," he said again.

She was looking at me, like doctors do when letting you know the visit is over. I struggled into my coat, which seemed to take forever, while she smiled coldly at me and said Goodbye.

Martin smiled.

I noticed he wasn't tall and even had a stomach, an old man, and I began to think about kissing her goodbye but why bother, it would be like trying to kiss a mannequin, and he said Goodbye again in that deep voice, and I smiled at him girlishly.

I couldn't feign being older with him, and I found myself walking down her orange-carpeted hallway to the elevator, as if I had just passed some important initiation rite, without knowing what it was.

* Nineteen

The woman with polio lay stretched out on her back. That was all she could do. She wore her hair mousy brown flipped up, but her lips were lit with a glossy pink lipstick. In other words, she had a joyous spirit underneath her brown batik sheet. She said, "So what are you up to these days?"

"Finishing school. Playing in the city."

She smiled. I was fingering her paintings. The colors were vibrant, pink, yellow, red, green, feminine.

"I did those on the porch of the cottage by the sea I go to summers. In Cape Cod. Truro. You would love it. You respond to beauty."

I thought about that. It was true. But why did I? Because beauty was uncomplicatedly pure. It gave me hope.

"Well?" she asked, watching me finger through the paintings.

"They're great."

"I get such pleasure—" she said.

I looked at her. Such pleasure. I loved music passionately. But was it enough to sustain me? No, I needed love too. I wondered how she could have such pleasure when she could not meander the streets, when no men's eyes were roaming around her.

"The sound of the sea. . . ." she was going on.

I nodded.

"You must go to the Cape," she said. "And come visit me. I sit outside on my porch and just take the beach in down below and the islands. It's all so rich," she added.

I stared at her.

Marilyn also never cried. She was dogged about getting dressed in the morning, no matter how badly her legs or arms refused to cooperate. She never volunteered what she felt and I regret to say I may not have asked, my confused universe choking up all the oxygen in my environment.

Still, I felt what she went through. I knew she accepted that her body made her different, made her unappealing to some. But she also had the assurance of being loved. Her family sent cards and letters and a continual trickle of food and little gifts, which she shared with me. They booked her holiday flights as soon as possible. I would listen silently to their letters, their encouragement. I would listen as a foreigner does to a new language.

When Martin did call me later that week, the conversation was very quick. It made me stand a bit taller in the dark convent phone box.

"This is Martin Sibley."

"Hi Martin Sibley."

He laughed. "Hi."

"How did you know what school I go to?" My voice seemed to echo in the wooden phone box.

"I asked your mother."

"Ah—"

"School going well?" he asked, perfunctorily.

I couldn't hear his deep voice because I was embarrassed. Everything was going fast.

"Yes. You?" I asked.

"Well these are my busy days. A lot to get out. I have to be here at the paper in the office all the time. So, want to have dinner on Friday or Saturday night?"

"Saturday," I said.

"Why don't you meet me at a restaurant in Westmount? It's called Elio's. It's on St. Catherine, near the library. You know where?"

"I know where the library is."

"You won't miss it then. Okay?"

He seemed to know that I did not stay at my mother's. He intuited how to put this date together.

That was that. The next day I snuck out of school for 15 minutes to buy the *Montreal Star* to look for his name. It was there. Martin Sibley. I showed his name to Ann McNichol, who sat beside me in study hall, and told her I was going out with him. She thought I was joking.

In bed, I said to Marilyn, "Can you believe I am going on a date with the editor of the *Montreal Star*?"

Marilyn foghorned out, "Isn't he old?"

"Of course he's old but he knows things. He's probably wise."

She didn't comment.

"He's very masculine," I explained. "It will be interesting to know him. I'll get help growing up."

✳ Twenty

Elio's turned out to be in his neighborhood, which was a ritzy part of Westmount, two or three story houses with lawns and gardens.

It was an unusually warm night. Everyone was outside, shorn of their coats and fingering their bare throats and necks in amazed delight, taking advantage of the warmth because, in this country, it was more than likely it would ice and snow tomorrow.

When he met me on the street, he asked if I minded if three of us had dinner, for he was standing with his giant airedail on a leash. It was really his son's dog, he said. He didn't reveal whether he was still married or divorced. True, dogs don't talk, I said to myself as we walked a few blocks looking for an outdoor cafe where we could sit with the dog, but still. It would be too much of a giveaway that he is married, this having a dog, so only someone with the confidence of not being married would bring their dog.

I was a bit surprised that he had a dog.

We found a pretty cafe with tables on a patio and Martin introduced me to a couple he knew sitting there, which I found very grown up, and once we had all exclaimed about the unseasonably warm weather, the other man devouring me with his eyes, which I found reassuring and hoped Martin noticed, and the wife looking impatient, another couple sitting next to the table we were to be seated at said to Martin, "You're not bringing that dog in here, are you?" and I piped up, "It'll just sit quietly," but Martin agreed and moved the dog to the outside of the deck.

Martin was very charming asking me what I wanted to eat, ordered for us both (it was Japanese) and here again he threw me another curve ball. "It's pleasant," he said, "not being on a complicated date."

"What do you mean?"

"I mean you clearly don't have two ex husbands and one emotionally disturbed child. We're just having dinner."

"Do you have two ex wives?"

"No just one. And one successful son and one emotionally disturbed son who goes constantly to discotheques."

"A mistress?"

He looked up from his glasses. "I have a mistress, yes."

This is where he would begin about my mother. I sat up a bit taller.

"What is she like?" I asked.

"She's the only woman I have ever met who is more sexual than me. Very independent. The exact opposite of you in that she is 61. But she looks fantastic. Wasp bones. Anyway she now wants to get married. She's ready. Not to me necessarily but she wants to settle down."

He's even cheating on my mother.

"Maybe she doesn't really want to," I replied. "Maybe she doesn't really want to settle down."

He looked at me questioningly.

"I mean if she hasn't already," I said.

He nodded and smiled.

I must be some kind of a sounding board for him, I decided. It was safe, in its own way, exactly where I liked to be.

"You know with sex—you'll find out—" he said, "that you have a loop of eroticism but if there's no emotional connection then it gets, well—"

"Repetitive?"

"Right."

I nodded, very understandingly.

He said he was starting a book, even while being at the paper. He needed time for that, he said coldly.

I nodded.

He told me he loved my looks and later he told me that he loved talking to me (I couldn't figure out why except that I was quiet). He didn't ask me much about myself, which in its way was relieving.

After dinner he suggested we take a walk in Westmount Park with his dog. I liked that idea too. It was odd to be doing these wholesome things with this man whom I decided must be decadent, because he seemed so pleased with himself.

We walked and the evening was pretty, with a pink sunset and trees shyly budding thin fleshy green. The dog was tame and not interested in other dogs (what did that say about Martin? I wondered) or in me (did the dog find me deficient in some way?).

Martin said things like, "The French seem to have figured out a way to make marriage palatable. They live their own materialistic lives within it."

"Unlike Tristan and Isolde," I said.

He laughed.

"The French," I said, "are practical."

"They treat marriage as a business arrangement, you're right. But maybe it is. You see women have more to give up in marriage. Women are objects of desire. Who wants to give up being that?"

I took all this in.

How could a woman of 61 be an object of desire? I was at the age where a woman of 21 was old.

"Well," I said, "I probably won't get married."

He smiled at me. "That's a good idea."

We were just crossing back to the road when he told me that there was a young guy staying at his place, a guy from Italy, who had everything, looks, brains, wanted to bring about world peace, all of it, and he'd love me to meet him.

I was confused that now he wanted me to meet some young guy. Did he actually feel paternal towards me? Was I wrong and this was a wholesome guy? But what about the way he kept looking at me when he thought I wasn't noticing it. Anyway, I didn't feel like meeting anyone. Something had still not transpired between Martin and me although I was not sure what I expected. He couldn't possibly have called me up to be a sounding board. Or maybe men did things like that.

We walked to his house, which was very near the Park. It turned out he owned one of the big houses in Westmount. He said that with the French scaring all the English out of Quebec, real estate prices were cheap and he could afford life among the bourgeoisie.

Yet, he must want to be one of the bourgeoisie to live with the bourgeoisie, which didn't bode well for us. Still . . . he made me very curious. It was the constant element of surprise with him. Nothing was as I expected.

We passed through a gate and the house was, when I got inside, completely clean. "The maid just came today," he said. The inside of the house was ultra modern with abstract paintings and Picasso drawings and chrome tables. There were a few watercolors of naked women by Martin himself and some Egon Schieles of people in erotic positions that he had cut out of art books scotch taped up here and there.

When we were in his hallway, he forgot all about the Italian young man he wanted to introduce me to. Just as I had thought. Did he think he needed such a boorish lure?

He said, "Want to see my bunker?"

"Okay," I said.

We walked down some stairs to a book lined study which had many records neatly lined up on shelves. "What would you like to hear?" he asked.

"You choose."

He put on some rhythmic guitar with drums.

He said, "Come sit over here."

He was sitting on a couch.

I moved over to him.

At first, he put his arm around me and I lay back on his chest while we silently listened to the music. I was trying to feel comfortable in the strangeness. He began rubbing my breasts, which were braless under a gray t-shirt. I had worn pearls with the t-shirt to give myself some class.

He pulled the t-shirt up and began fondling my breasts. That was something I loved, when a man did that. I felt full, womanly, expansive. I felt more substantial. My breasts were bigger than my mother's, although hers were supposedly nice. She had told me that. That her lovers liked her breasts.

He brought his mouth down to my nipples. This felt edgy. He sighed and said, "I would give up the 61-year-old for you."

Power. Mine.

He was fondling me and I wanted to say Stop but I found myself, of all things, becoming the aggressor. I turned and knelt on the couch and began kissing him. I closed my eyes because he was so old. Then he lay me back down on the couch and began kissing my upper stomach. I moved him on top of me and I could feel his hard on and I began to move. I felt flushed. We were bumping and grinding in our clothes.

"There could be a more comfortable, pleasurable way to do this," he said in that deep voice.

He unzipped my slacks and pushed them down. This I had never let a man do before. But somewhere I had decided that tonight was going to be a departure from what I did before. I was tired of all that I had been doing before.

I wanted to go blank, like you do with drink, and with everything else when you concentrate hard. I wanted to forget, although I did not know what.

I just thought, Oh fuck it.

He pushed into me, and it stung a bit at first, but then it seemed to get slicker and he began moaning and caressing me and sort of dancing, it seemed, inside me and I was trying to get the rhythm down, I was caught in wanting to dance with him, so I feigned the dance movements of hip to hip but I just liked him, the masculinity of him, on top of me and in me and then he said, Oh God, and he gripped the top of my head hard and squeezed my head into my shoulders and he gasped, Oh God.

After that, I felt all warm and soft inside. He waited a minute and said, "Next time we'll get you to say, Oh God."

✳ Twenty-One

I sat in the Bistro the next day wondering when Martin would call me, and why had I chosen him?

I looked around. There was that woman in the bar I always saw. That older woman, older than my mother, or not as well preserved.

She smiled at me rather sweetly.

I stood up, for I was always in motion, and walked over to her.

"I heard you tell the bartender you have a boyfriend," she said.

"Well, I slept with someone," I replied, sitting down.

"That can be considered a boyfriend."

"I don't think he is."

She said nothing, then she said, "Yes, at your age people just sleep together."

"Well, actually, he's more your age." I instantly regretted saying that.

Her face looked for a tiny millisecond as if it had been hit and then she said, making sure her voice did not betray she had been hurt, "And you like him?"

I thought for a moment. "I don't know."

Then I said creatively, "He's probably a bad sort," I said, "going for someone so much younger, like me. He probably has a weak character."

She laughed at this ridiculous attempt at kindness and then she did a strange thing. She put her creamed hand over mine, she was wearing one rather small marquise diamond on her finger, so small that it looked like it must have been given to her in another time, when her life had been smaller, more innocent, and she said, "Don't let them take everything."

"No," I said, although I did not know what she meant.

"Have you finished school?" she asked.

"Almost."

"You are bright, I am sure."

"Why do you say that?"

"You are very alive."

I played with my hair. I didn't like my haircut. It seemed too clean cut for me; some idiot had given me a blunt cut. I was trying to muss it up, get that bedridden look.

"What will you do after?" she asked.

"After?"

"School."

"Work, I suppose."

Now she looked sad again. "Ah," she said, "you are alone. I thought so. I am too. We are the ones who take solace in work. We hide there." Now she clicked her lips going ts ts ts ts as if I, or we, were doing something wrong.

I didn't see anything wrong with working. It seemed like an adventure to me.

"I'll be independent," I said. "Have my own place."

She looked at me sadly again.

Then the door blew open and I looked over annoyed at someone holding the damn door open too long in this ice chill, and there poured in Jim Lawrence carrying bags.

Good God, what was he doing here?

"I thought I'd find you," he said. "You're disturbingly easy to track down. I just flew in from Toronto."

He nodded to the woman. "This is. . . ?" I said.

"Annick," she said and she held out her hand.

"Hello Annick. Listen," he said to me, "can we speak alone for a minute?"

"Sure," I said. I motioned to her that I had to go, she nodded again and smiled, and I was glad to get away. She was so sad.

"Let's sit down here," I said.

"Okay."

He ordered a coffee with no alcohol. "Listen," he said," are you okay about the other night? There are quite a few ramifications."

"You mean the other night with you?"

"Yes. Why? What other types of nights have you been up to?"

"I don't know."

"Have you told your mother?"

"About going drinking with you?"

"Yes and sleeping at my place. I think maybe we should keep this little bit to ourselves. It's not really her business."

"Anyway . . . you don't have to worry," I answered. "I'm not chasing you or anything. I see other guys."

"You should. You should see guys your own age."

"Well . . . I like guys, men I mean. I mean I even like one who is older than you."

"Another friend of your mother's?"

"Yes. Do you know Martin Sibley?"

Jim looked over darkly at me. "You know Martin? Of course I know him. Everybody knows him."

"He's nice, isn't he?"

I thought Jim would be impressed with my dating someone who in essence could be his boss. Maybe I could help Jim's career.

Jim said, "Well, I wouldn't say nice. He's I guess nice if you give him what he wants."

"What do you mean?"

"He goes through a lot of women. But he's smart. Very smart."

"Well you go through a lot of women too."

"Not that many. Anyway . . . you're too young for him."

Being young, I decided at that moment, is to be constantly underestimated.

"Anyway I wanted to check up on you," he said.

"You don't have to," I said.

"I know. But," he put his arm around me, "you're kind of cute."

Somebody cared about me. In that moment, I felt my life was happy. Maybe it wasn't unsafe. I was in demand everywhere. Someone might find me.

"You know," he said, "that this thing is not," he stroked his hair, "unconnected to your mother. On your part," he said.

"What thing?"

"I mean, between you and me. Or Martin which I hope is not true. It's not usual."

"Well neither is she," I said.

"Your attraction to me may not be about me," he said.

Why was he so sure I was attracted to him? After all, he must have serious personality flaws, liking my mother. And I had obviously been more attracted to Martin. To not hurt Jim's feelings, for God knows I knew about hurt feelings, I said, "I like you for you. I know what I'm doing."

"Okay," he said kindly, "I believe you believe that you like me for me." He had finished his coffee. "I want to go back to my place and relax."

He got up. I held onto my cognac. He looked at me.

"Well?" he said.

"Well what?"

"Do you want to come?"

"Oh," I said, "I didn't know you wanted me to." And then I got my things and did up my yellow coat and George the Hungarian sculptor was watching us with his back to us through the bar mirror. He nodded as I left. I smiled goodbye to Annick and she nodded, but she didn't smile. I felt confused, like I was leaving my home to go off with a man but this time perhaps, perhaps I was going to some other kind of home.

✳ Twenty-Two

Martin hadn't called. I interpreted this as an act of willful aggression against me. He was choosing not to call.

Maybe I'd visit my mother and she would let slip some information. Or maybe I'd even meet a new man there. Already I had learned that one man could distract one's feelings from the other. I decided to go over to her place.

I trudged over there, sad. It was something female, I sensed. Some way of having been touched and made needy and vulnerable and then having to live with it.

Maybe I would discuss it with her. She knew a lot about this. However when my mother came out of the bedroom dressed in a wool skirt and brown silk shirt, she looked like she didn't want to hear about my problems. Oddly, she sat down very close to me. I moved away. She came in closer and put her head on my shoulder. "Stroke my hair," she said. "I love when someone strokes my hair."

I did, reluctantly. I wanted to talk but she seemed as if she was on her own mission.

"That is so good," she said.

I could smell the musty smell again. Now I knew it was sex. I was not sure who had visited her before me.

She was staring out the window.

"I just took some pills," she said. "Etienne was a cheat. You know that. Jim is a playboy. Alvin is a fool. I am so sick of it—they contribute nothing. They're incapable of love—all I ever wanted was to be in love. I am a romantic," she said. "But these men, these men are unable to give."

I had heard this speech many times before on other desultory afternoons. I was bored. In fact, it seemed like it was the only thing we talked about. Men.

"What do you think of Martin?" I asked very casually.

"He's intelligent. He likes women. If a woman is after him, he always responds. Men are very opportunistic that way. They can't resist a woman who responds to them. It has nothing to do with the woman. Keep stroking my hair, dahling."

Then I remembered. "What do you mean by pills?" I asked. I felt numb as I asked her. It would be such a burden off me if she would just go away. Numb, as if I had taken the pills myself.

"I took them earlier. I don't want to live. I'm just sick of it."

Was this possible?

"How do you feel now?" I asked.

She didn't answer and just lay her head heavier on me. Then she put her small hand into mine. It felt limp, but then it always did.

"Be my mummy," she said in a little girl voice.

I was horrified.

I didn't believe this pill business. It just seemed like more drama. Or, if she had taken them, she seemed pretty clear to me. I felt like a murderer by not being upset if she had taken them. In fact, I seemed to almost hope she had. But maybe I could hope that because deep down I was sure she hadn't.

I woodenly put my arm around her.

I felt very rational.

"I feel normal," she said, finally.

I was stroking her brittle dyed red hair. "Mummy," she said in a child's voice, meaning me. "Mummy," she said again.

I grimaced an encouraging smile.

These pills, or whatever they were, did not seem to be working.

❋ Twenty-Three

My mother slept off her pills and returned to her life, her job at the Film Board and to seeing Alan when she went to London. I didn't see much of her, being busy now with my own life.

For me, Montreal was softening. It was early Spring and the mountain was full of pink and white flowering trees and the big avenues like Sherbrooke and Ste Catherine were lit by pale gentle flowering buds during the day and gas lights by night.

I still walked, hoping to "accidentally" run into Martin. I had already walked up and down Guy and Crescent and Mountain, not that I had ever seen him there to begin with. Now I veered toward Old Montreal. I passed the space age buildings of Place des Arts where the Montreal Symphony played their difficult modern French composers and Gordon Lightfoot sang heroically of the Canadian Railroad.

I was walking all over the place. I thought walking the city randomly might bring something about.

I passed the wrought iron graceful gates to the McGill University campus. All those University houses lit up like British estates, with curving pathways running between them. They looked like castles in fairy tales. The buildings were sturdy and, if you went there, you became sturdy yourself.

I hadn't made any real effort to apply to college. College, I had told myself, was the refuge of the bourgeois. I would be an artist, a writer maybe or something once my talent clicked in, but in the meantime I would do what all great artists did, I would live on the edge.

My father once said, "I never see you writing if you want to be a writer," but I thought this was his usual pedantic thinking. What great writer goes about writing in front of people? My plan was just to be great when I settled down into that phase of my life. Meanwhile, I would follow my desire pressing along the streets. This, I rationalized, was the true training ground of the artistic.

I didn't know that, having been schooled in bars and with a mother who made me feel I did not have the right to belong, that I felt too shy or embarrassed to go to a college. I didn't know that then.

I finally hit Old Montreal and felt small and useless amid all those huge gray stone fortresses. This was a different world than manicured English-speaking Westmount.

These were authoritarian political buildings. Buildings full of French people angry at the country they live in, wanting to form their own country, people fighting for a cause. The cafes were full of separatists, revolutionaries. I myself had read revolutionary writers, like Fanon, Marx, Mao, not always understanding what I was reading, but in deep sympathy with the thinking that you had to act forcefully, impersonally (and here I got a bit nervous, was this not how my mother acted toward me?), you had to not put your own feelings first, but those of the collective, and you had to destroy the cancers within society.

The cancer in Montreal at that time, in the sixties, was the English. Quebec would separate as a socialist state. I hung about the Spanish Club, an upstairs bodega, where revolutionaries met. I would sit at the edge of their big tables while they smoked cigarettes and in a feverish pitch discussed subtleties of manifestos. These men did not try to pick me up, having a higher calling.

Jim Lawrence lived near the Spanish Club and, sometimes, afterward, I would go over there. Sometimes Jim let me stay at his apartment when he was unexpectedly called off to some other province to cover something.

He never tried to sleep with me again. He was a decent sort. An anomaly, I thought.

"How can you not wear any stockings in this cold?" he asked when I dropped by. "It's still too cool to go about in bare legs. Were you at the Spanish Club?"

"Yes." I lit a cigarette.

"Quite a team your mother and you. She's talking the benefits of a Canadian Government pension and you're planning on blowing up some Minister."

"I might join a revolutionary theatre, and play Jackie Kennedy or something. A Genet play where the underlings are under the stage. We plan to put dummies of people in the audience and walk through and punch them. To unnerve the bourgeoisie."

He stared through me.

"What else are you up to?" he asked.

"Martin Sibley, the journalist—"

Jim looked quickly up.

"—mentioned a screen test, when we had that dinner. Although I can't act. I'm going to call him. He said he'd come over and read scripts with me."

"He probably has other things in mind."

"I'm going to get an apartment. Somewhere cheap around McGill. I have to ask my father for the down payment."

"So you're off and running."

"Yes."

Jim would put on music, maybe even Theoderakis, with whom I had begun a great musical attachment to because he was a revolutionary like me. We would sit in the dark, listening and speaking in low voices.

"Are you still seeing her?" I asked.

"Yes," he'd laugh.

My drive to connect with him was mildly flirtatious, but not really erotic. I wanted him to just be there, caring for me, and make no demands. My erotic fire was channeled into walking, into attracting, into perhaps bonding with Martin Sibley or Martin Sibley facsimiles and their manly taking. But Martin had not called and, when I roamed the Westmount streets, I did not find him. Maybe Jim did not reject me enough for me to get that feeling of desire, that feeling I had been born to.

Before Jim left for work, I often would suggest he report on the inevitable revolution. Like a journalist, Jim would ask the names of all the places I went to hear the talk and some of the plans they had. I was just at the fringes of the malcontents. I never was in the Federation Liberation Quebec, the group who believed in killing ministers or bombings. He took notes but he never followed up on them. He was chasing what his station told him to.

I graduated from high school and transferred my time to a waitressing job at a local cafe and being outdoors on spring days. I rarely saw my mother.

One time I went with Jim in his old car to the Laurentian mountains. I rode beside Jim in thrall at this sensual luxury of being in a car, seeing new sights. We stopped off for lunch outdoors on the rolling lawn of a sprawling French hotel, with the big Canadian trees around us, just listening to an icy brook running quickly nearby and the shiny black Canadian birds calling out with piercing clarity to each other. I was sure he preferred being with me to being with her, for the delicacy of it.

I thought he and I were alike. We both needed the toughness, the erotic toughness of a person like my mother or Martin Sibley because we were not the using type; we were not the type of people who just looked out for ourselves. We were people who cared. Martin and my mother were more types who did well in the world, didn't get hurt. They did the hurting. Jim and I were softer and it was sadder, but nicer. That's what I thought. And, even then, I knew there was not much to do about it.

✳ Twenty-Four

I came home to my new apartment that my father had lent me the down payment for. My father had $900 in his checking account and had willingly written out a check for $850 to the landlords. His hand trembled as he did it, but he said, "Of course I'll help you."

I came home to my new apartment and the phone rang and it was Martin. All charming, "been so busy" and "missed you" and "I must see you," and did I want to see an erotic French film in Old Montreal? I had never been to a French or any other language erotic film.

"Okay."

All felt right now with the order of things, now that he was finally showing interest in me. This was how it was supposed to be with men and women.

I was reprieved from his rejection.

The film played in an old gray building with a plush vestibule with rich red velvet drapes, which you went through into a small theatre. We snuggled into each other when the lights went out and I watched young bodies, like my own, writhe on top of each other, have orgasm after orgasm, which I had not yet had with a man, only with myself, which I now wanted to do, squirming in my seat.

I wanted to reach my hand into my pants to relieve this tension and I could tell that Martin, with his heavy breathing, and his hands going quicker and quicker round my breasts, my stomach, between my legs, in the dark, wanted to give me an orgasm too.

Soon his hand was in my pants and I lifted my body so he could put his hand on my clitoris. It was not difficult. The movie had me almost there. He brought me to orgasm. Then he brought my hand to his penis but I didn't know how to do what he wanted so I stroked it, unzipped his trousers, brought it up, lost interest, it went down, back up, but I was too embarrassed to exert the pressure to make him come. After ten minutes or so, he put his hand over mine and began to move my hand faster, and when I was rough, he told me to be gentle, and when I was gentle, he told me to go harder, and soon he was breathing quietly in sort of gasps. I passed him a napkin I had brought in for my coke.

When the movie was over, which was incredibly boring no matter what damn language it was in, he dispensed with the dinner idea and said, Let's go back to my place.

At sixteen, I was at an age where I went along with everything. He unlocked his door brusquely and never taking his hands off, it seemed, my breasts and bottom, managed to pull me by my arms into his bunker, as he had called it, not his bedroom.

And there he undressed me and I wanted to star in this porno movie in his mind. It was only minutes before I was riding him backwards, up and down and he was going Oh God oh God and I too, a wave came over me, such a wave, that I suddenly heard and felt my timid voice, be not so timid, grunting and breathing hard, escaping me, while pushing down hard on him as I had my first orgasm with a man inside me.

When I had come, I hung my head down, embarrassed. I avoided looking at him.

Martin, conversely, was smiling and telling me that I was coming along well. He jumped up, energized, but couldn't find anything in the refrigerator and suggested we order in pizza.

All I knew was I wanted to get away. This being vanquished in front of a man. Having a feeling. I didn't like it. I didn't know what had happened to me, this woman whose body did things without my permission.

And, anyway, what was there to talk about?

"I have to get ready for my waitressing job," I suddenly said, busily dressing. "I should go." I couldn't wait to get out of there. And return to the one person I somewhat trusted, myself.

He tried to hide his pleasure in my wanting to leave and said, "Oh of course. I understand."

He walked me to the door, his hairy stomach hanging out, and he said, "I'll call you," at the same time that I said, "I'll call you."

We laughed and I raced out, tingling but excited, anxious, to be alone. He shut the door quickly behind me.

But when I got out into the night, I didn't really want to be alone. I wanted to feel safe, be held by some familiar warmth. I wanted to be with people who might care for me. I wanted to talk about, even without words, what I had just been through.

I called her.

"Dahling," she said on the phone, "I'm busy right now."

"I see."

"Well perhaps we can all meet," she said. "Jim and I are going to have a late dinner. You can come over."

I knew what dinner would be. Cold cuts, a meager salad, German bread, and some wine. (This was what she always served, never a cooked meal, not that I cared.) However, I was hungry so I was willing to eat the requisite salami and liverwurst.

Jim acted happy to see me, and she was in a good mood with Jim there and with the odd occurrence of me seeming to be pleased I was there. As if perhaps maybe we did all get along.

She had a distinctly stylish way. The way the roped mats were set, the dishes. The slim stemmed glasses for the wine.

We were sitting down at the table.

"How is school?" she asked.

"I graduated."

"Oh? When?"

"A month ago."

She looked at me trying to remember if I had told her this. She was not Americanized enough to know that this was an event to make a fuss over. School was over, that was all. For a second, I wanted her to ask me about Marilyn.

"Did I mention—" I said, "that I had this roommate who has cerebral palsy?"

"No," she said. "How weird."

"I don't think she's going back next year. She missed her family or maybe they missed her too much."

I was curious to see how that would go over. She just looked at me as if to say, what are you talking about?

"Anyway it was sad how she had to struggle, you know, but she did."

"Where are you living now?" my mother said, not interested in this type of sentimentality.

"I told you," I said. "I'm living on Stanley and waitressing at the Cafe Pamplona."

"That's all you're doing?"

"Well I'm looking for a real job."

Jim piped up, "Why don't you get her a job at the Film Board?"

"That would be nepotism," she said.

I was noticing how life soon returns to normal after having sex.

"So what?" he said. "She likes movies. She could start as a script girl."

"You would have to be responsible," she said to me, "not show up stoned on drugs." Something my mother thought I did all the time. However, I didn't.

Jim said, "I don't know. Plenty of them do."

She laughed as it was coming from him. "I wonder if you could be a secretary to the production," she said.

"What would I do?"

"Get coffee for the director and assistant director," she said. "They'll tell you. It's not difficult."

I felt a little embarrassed about working in her world. She might get to know me. Although obviously I didn't feel embarrassed about sleeping with someone in her world.

"How's your father?" she asked.

"He's writing a book."

"It will never be published."

"Probably not," I said.

"He has no insight."

Jim asked, "You haven't been about much lately. Do you have a boyfriend?"

Lisbeth said, "It's odd, isn't it? She never has one. What's wrong with her?" she asked him.

"Maybe she's choosey."

"Even being choosey," my mother said, "she should be able to find someone."

"I see people," I ventured.

"You always say that, but you're so vague about it."

"Have you seen Martin?" Jim asked.

"A bit."

"You're seeing Martin?" she asked.

"He takes me to a movie or so."

Jim said to her, "I thought you were seeing Martin also."

"He takes me to a movie or so, too," she replied, laughing. "I guess everyone is seeing Martin. Do you ever see anyone your own age?" she turned to me.

"No. I don't meet people my own age."

"She's in bars all the time. There are no young people there. As young as her I mean," he said.

"It's her father," my mother said. "He's ruined her."

I helped myself to more bread. I had another glass of wine.

"Well if you meet someone who has a girlfriend," my mother said, "it means nothing. All my husbands left their wives for me. They say men don't leave but they do. I should write a book on how to get a man to leave the woman he is with. How to steal him. It probably would be very successful."

I thought, how vulgar.

She was now looking at me, "You just have to be firm about wanting him, reassure him. You just have to be very clear and of course very sexy."

What does she mean by sexy anyway? I asked myself. What is it they all do and they all like so much? I knew the part about our bodies getting all heated up kissing and rubbing up against each other, how insistent that all was, toward completion, but what was this mysterious sexy she always talked about? "He was." "She was."

I looked to Jim. Then he said, "Maybe she doesn't want this man to leave whomever he's with."

At that, I realized Jim thought he was the man in my life.

"Do you?" she asked.

"I don't know," I said. "I don't know him that well."

"Well the other woman must be older than you."

"Yes," I said.

"Some men like older women," she said. "Older women are far more interesting and even more attractive."

I shrugged, wondering if I was supposed to be pleased at this news.

She patted my hand, "If this doesn't work, the next one will."

I dragged on my cigarette. I was still focused on what was sexy. Was there some secret the initiated knew that I didn't? Should I have moved my body in a different way?

This subject was making me uncomfortable. I really wanted to discuss Martin but I knew she and Jim weren't the people to discuss it with. Maybe she liked Martin. I stood up and started looking for a jacket I hadn't brought. I made a great show, for Jim's benefit, of taking off my sweater, while looking for this jacket, tucking in my shirt, smoothing my pants, jumping up and down from the couch to chair to chair just to be sure that the room was full of me.

I saw her watching me.

"Where are you going?" Jim asked.

"Oh she's probably going to a bar," my mother said.

"Are you?" he asked.

I was but I didn't answer in order to be mysterious.

"Or a movie," I said. "Have you seen Baiser Moi?"

"The French porno film?" my mother asked.

"Yes."

"Who would want to see that?" she asked. "I find those things so boring."

As I put my cardigan back on, my mother said, "It would be nice if you met someone, darling. You shouldn't be so alone. You need somebody to take care of you."

Yes, I thought.

I checked my paper bag to make sure it had my lipstick, brush and $20. I thought purses too middle class so I carried a paper bag, you could always get a new one, when Jim said, "Are you alright? You seem unusually distracted."

"She's always distracted," from her.

"I am a bit," I said. "I don't know why."

"She'll be alright," my mother said. Why was no one talking to me? "She's young. They get through everything."

I looked over at her to perhaps begin to argue the point but I saw her kissing the top of Jim's head.

What I would be, I decided, walking along outside, was I would be on the outside. People have fewer expectations, I told myself, when you're on the outside and you can be anyway you want. And, obviously, no one can hurt you. I must stay on the outside. And not get close to anyone.

✻ Twenty-Five

My father returned from Toronto, now that the writing business had not worked out. He was seeing, as he said, what was about.

It made me sad to think of this big lonely old man, overweight and out of synch from drink, looking for work. They must treat him as a dinosaur, I assumed. Another

Englishman landed in Canada, mistakenly thinking it was the land of wheat and honey. Instead it was just the land of wheat. But I was sure some sales manager would eventually bet on him solely for his public school British accent. An accent which always sounds knowledgeable, no matter what the hell it is going on about.

But that day I had other things on my mind, as we sat at the Cavalier.

"Can you believe that Martin and Jim truly like Lisbeth?" I asked my father.

"Well they don't know her."

"I never hear from Martin or Jim. It's peculiar."

"Why should you? They're HER boyfriends, I hope."

"Well, they liked me in their way too."

"What has that got to do with anything?" he said, taking a swig of his drink.

"How could they just forget about me just like that? They used to like to spend time with me."

"Stop talking about *they*. *They* can't be the same person," he said.

"Okay," I said. "Well the Martin one liked to take me to dinner, even a movie. Now he doesn't call."

"Maybe this Martin guy doesn't like anyone. Maybe he'd just rather be alone."

I thought maybe here my father had moved onto talking about himself.

"Lisbeth doesn't lead a half bad life, you know," I said, not sure if I was saying it to get a rise out of him or because I believed it.

"Neither does anyone. You can always live a better one."

"I don't know how."

He didn't respond. He put his glass to his lips, held it there before swallowing and turned his eyes away from me and said, "Work at a decent job and meet someone decent."

"I don't know how to meet someone decent," hoping he didn't hear the teary edge in my voice.

"It'll happen."

"I don't think it'll happen to me."

"Don't be ridiculous."

Jeanette turned to us, away in her own world of moving bottles behind the bar into some kind of order that only she would understand, and said, "It's good to have your father back, ay?"

I nodded again but I was intent on my theme with him. "I don't think anything good will happen to me. I think I'll end up here forever," I said waving to the mirror and bottles of the Cavalier bar.

"Well what's wrong with that?" he asked.

I left him to go find a job. I went down to wide, wealthy, business-like Avenue Rene Levesque to apply for two secretarial jobs, one at the Bank of Montreal corporate headquarters and, the other, at the Queen Elizabeth Hotel. At the bank, my pink dress rode up to my thighs when the head of personnel interviewed me. I pulled it down to sit on the chair but I saw the woman interviewer watch me do that. I didn't get the job. Nor the one at the Queen Elizabeth Hotel.

I began to worry about how to support myself. Would I have to buy a non-descript suit and answer some office telephone? Stay put from 9 to 5, befriend people in offices and care about them like family until I went to the next job? Where do all the misfits go, I wondered? To serve food in restaurants? Drive cabs? I would need a boyfriend because it would be too hard alone.

I continued this pursuit for a new job but sometimes I just couldn't leave my apartment. I knew that people were able to see just by looking at me that I was intrinsically all wrong. They could see I lacked courage to enter their world. I was failing, tiring of the bars, and finding it exhausting to find the entryway into a so-called real world. Tiring, and not yet seventeen. Already the whole thing seemed repetitious.

I was feeling all that, while sitting on my couch looking out the big picture window at the other apartment buildings on Peel, only to hear the woman on the telephone tell me that, "Yes dear, that's correct. It's positive."

I was pregnant.

I hadn't thought of that. I hadn't thought it would happen to me. I was young enough to believe just willing it not to happen meant it wouldn't.

Pregnant.

By Martin.

I wasn't going to tell him. It was my fault. My body. My future.

So I found myself sitting in my mother's large office at the Film Board.

She took a phone call while I sat across from her. She did not look at me.

"Well what is it you want?"

"Could I borrow money?" I asked. I wanted to ask her first. She was the one who wouldn't feel the loan.

"For what?"

"An abortion."

"You're pregnant?"

I nodded.

"Can't you ask the father?"

"I don't want to."

"Why not? He's the father."

"There is no father because there is no baby."

"I know," she said, "you are not the type to have a child."

Was that a compliment coming from her? Or did she have us confused?

"No, I don't want to ask the father. It's, it's none of his business really if I'm having an abortion."

"What?" she asked.

"Well I don't think he'd care. I mean—I don't even like him. I don't want to ask him."

"You're so peculiar," she said.

We sat in silence for a minute, a long minute, and then she said, "Why are you crying?"

I was crying so much I couldn't see her.

"I don't know."

"There's something wrong with you," she said. "Who is the father?"

"A man I know. I just said he wouldn't want to help me. It was not a big thing. He was just . . . he was just . . . using. . . . "

"Well can't you just use him? Get the money from him?"

When, I wanted to know, do we skip to the kindness part? How could I answer these questions? I had waterfall answers. Boats of answers that would bump down Niagara Falls. That's where my answers were.

Anyway I was still crying, and I knew this crying was not about two hundred dollars.

Her dark eyes looked at me trying to understand what to do with me.

She had the advantage. I was beside myself.

She continued, "Perhaps you should see a psychiatrist. You seem to be crazy."

I knew she had had abortions when she was my age. Why was I so deserving of condemnation?

"I don't have as much money as you think," she said. "Gerald always exaggerates how much money I make . . . "

I stood up. I could see I wasn't going to get the money. I didn't know why I tried.

"And then," she said, "I want to go see Alan in England. I must see him every year and I'm the one who pays because of his wife . . . "

I began waving my long slender hands because I was still crying, I waved my hands to say forget about it, forget about me, I shouldn't have asked, I shouldn't have come, forget about me, don't even look at me, don't see me, don't look at how lost I am, go back to the imaginary movie camera. Pretend this never happened. I was waving my hands.

She sat looking at me with annoyance, as if I was a strange thing. There was nothing to do but turn around, and destined for loneliness, I walked out of her office and down the hallways of her office building. People looked at me crying but what did it matter? This was who I really was.

Finally I was outside and hailed a cab with the little tip money I had. I would have to find Martin and ask for the money or ask someone else.

I took the cab home through the wet snowy streets full of 1950s square apartment buildings that looked as if the lives lived there were as difficult as mine and finally I got back downtown to where the buildings were ornate and wealthy looking and the streets gave a feeling of promise, and I went in through my lobby and lay down on my bed.

There was no point in going anywhere.

✳ Twenty-Six

"Daddy, there's a lot of things going on."

"Like what?"

"Like I need 200 dollars."

"Alright," he said. He looked over at me cannily and slowly began pulling money out of his wallet.

"Maybe 250," I said.

"I thought you were working."

"Things come up."

"They do," he agreed.

I realized he didn't want to know and I respected that.

I kissed him and took a sip of his vodka and told him I'd call him.

"Call me here," he said. He meant the Cavalier Motel house phone.

"I know," and I went back home to make a different kind of phone call.

I booked the abortion for Friday.

Now that I was pregnant by Martin, I didn't want to see or talk to him, not that he was calling. I just didn't want to be reminded of my vulnerability. My body. My mind. I refused to think about the abortion. I told myself I could go through anything if I didn't think about it.

I was slightly proud that I had got pregnant, proof that I was female, but I could not imagine having a child. I couldn't imagine it, ever. I did not know why I couldn't. I did not know that I only associated pain with childhood.

But having got the money for the abortion briefly made me feel that I could surmount difficulties. So I decided to take a walk down Mountain towards Ste. Catherine, admire the elegant shops and reassure myself by my image in shop windows. I decided to stop in an expensive jewelry store to try on the sapphire and emerald rings set in heavy gold settings. I was looking at engagement rings to myself. Not that I could afford one. I was just looking. The owner slowly came out from behind the retail area, Hans someone or other the business card said, and yes these were his designs, he said slowly, as he looked me over even more slowly.

He told me that it seems we live near each other. In that apartment high-rise near my apartment. Why don't I come to a party he was having just that evening?

I left there curious. Why not? I suited remote sensual men. That's what he seemed in his slow movements, his actor-like German accent.

I rang his buzzer in the large gold lobby and was let in. When the elevator opened to his modern apartment, it was full of people of all nationalities, drinking and laughing but Hans was nowhere to be seen. I was not sure he would remember me anyway.

I looked at all the people, checking to see who was looking at me, and there were a few glances, but nothing to hold me, and then I saw the older woman from the bar.

She was dressed simply in a pink sweater set and a brown skirt, with a gold choker with some African icon tied to her throat, perhaps one of Hans' necklaces, and she was listening quietly while smiling to some man who looked like he did not want to be talking to her. She was safer in the bar, I thought. She was out of her world here. Just like me. I did not know what to say to her here.

I felt lonely standing there and immediately took a drink off the tray being passed around and thought what I could do was check myself out in the ladies room, see if I still had a friend.

The door was open and I could see the mirrors in the bathroom even from a distance and as I went in I realized that there were three people taking a bath together, one of them, it turned out, was Hans.

"Ah . . . " he said, "the jewelry gazer. Come in, come into my party."

Maybe these people know how to be happier than I do. I began to fumble with my dress and stockings. Me who hated my body.

And quickly, before they could see all my flaws, although truth was they were too busy slyly looking at their own reflections in the mirror-tiled walls, I got into the bath to join Hans and the liquor and the other people and Hans soon began fondling me in the midst of the bubbles and the laughter, no one giving a damn about knowing the other person, and this, this was supposed to be wildness and I looked at Hans' tired eyes and the handsome gray brown hair on his chest and his sensual mouth and I could not make my mind up whether he was a man of appetites or a man of incredible indifference.

He was laughing and swiping at all our bodies and we were all proffering our bodies, for the warmth of the water mixed with the heat of the alcohol, and sometimes he submerged himself supposedly wittily as a sea thing frolicking in female skin and water and the funny thing was that I could not get over the incredible sadness.

Once I allowed that thought, there was no retrieving it, and so I slowly got out of the bath, who cares if they see my fucking body.

I woke up wanting to leave Montreal. If it was Hans now, what would I next find to assuage my loneliness?

The nurse said not to have sex after the abortion for two weeks.

"Okay," I said.

However, I put the abortion and myself right out of my mind. It was as if it didn't happen.

I went back out to the bistros and the Winston Churchill Pub on Mountain Street and Crescent, god forbid that I should miss any repartee, any being looked at, any hands touching me or voices talking to me, god forbid I should feel any of my own misery, of not being part of a family, even one to come, let me not think about it, and so it was I met Yves and John and when they told me I was beautiful and they really, really liked me, that seemed to be the way I could take care of myself. The nurse had told me to take care of myself. These men surely would be nicer to me than I knew how to be.

That was how I got pregnant the second time, while recovering from the first time. I didn't tell anyone and borrowed the money from Yves. He liked me more than John did and I said it was his. Perhaps it was. He offered to come with me but I could not understand why anyone would want to attend an event designed for annihilation. I thought you went through the hard stuff alone. Why involve another in your error? Life punishes you and you punish you.

Afterwards, on the small cot in the clinic, I woke crying. You wake up crying. Not from physical pain, but from loss. This is what death feels like. No negotiation. Over.

I went to the Pamplona. I went to the Bistro. The bartenders and the waiters bought me drinks. I made them feel good they said, when I smiled at them.

I called Marilyn in Winnipeg when I got home one night. Her mother said, "Oh yes, Jacqueline. How nice to hear from you."

Marilyn got on the phone but it was more difficult to understand her if you couldn't see her.

She asked me if I was in love and I said no.

"You?"

She just laughed and said she was thinking of going to law school.

But how could she practice?

She went on, "I would do research and real estate. That kind of thing. What are you going to do?"

I shook my head at the phone. "I don't know. I kind of have to deal with each day. There's no time to plan ahead. Each day," I went on, "each day takes all of my attention. I think all this mess, all this mess of my life; I'll turn it into something. I don't know. Maybe I'll write a movie."

She laughed like it was a joke.

"What happened to the old man?" she asked.

"Who?"

"You know," she foghorned, "The guy you went out with."

"Oh, oh Martin. I don't know. He must be back with his sixty-one year old. Maybe I'm too old for him now. I'm no longer in high school."

She didn't touch that.

"What about—" she asked.

"Jim? He's in Toronto a lot. He doesn't see my mother anymore. It must have ended. Maybe he has a girlfriend. I don't go over there."

Just like, I thought, I don't see you anymore. I had the horrible thought that soon even Marilyn and I would forget about each other and not talk anymore.

"You should write me," I said.

"I hate to write, you know that."

"Okay," I said, "I'll keep calling. Good luck with school."

"Good luck with your movie. Write one," she said, "don't be in one."

I laughed. "Right."

* Twenty-Seven

"I saw the x-rays," he said to me, sitting at the bar.

"But Daddy you can't read x-rays."

"Don't tell me what I can or can't do. You have no idea."

I turned to my drink and refused to navigate my way through this conversation. I decided to say nothing. He didn't want to discuss the truth.

"It's hard keeping up a pretense," he said after awhile, this dialogue opened as a peace offering. He was staring at his neat scotch, which I noticed he was not drinking with the usual abandon.

"What pretense?" I asked, annoyed. About his health or something else? I, looking at myself in the mirror, was clearly against all pretense.

"The pretense of having money," he said. "You have to in this country."

A feigning Marxist, I turned my head from him in disgust. Although the more I was alone, the more I saw you needed money. One's life seemed to be consumed in solving that problem. It seemed a ridiculous concern and yet it shaped everyone's destiny.

"You should marry for money," he said.

I put my nose further up. Even love now had to be commercialized.

"I have no interest in that," I said.

"You wouldn't."

"No I wouldn't," I said looking round the bar, thinking who has money anyway?

"Well you'll have a tough life."

"At least it'll have ethics."

"Oh," he laughed, holding onto his drink. "How wonderful. That's what you think. It will just be difficult."

"I want to fall in love."

"I notice you never do."

"You probably ruined me," I said.

"I didn't," he said. As if I was ruined, but someone else did it.

"Since you raised me, you're the most likely culprit."

"Well I'll be gone."

I took his long bony hand, that I loved so, and stroked it. "Don't say that."

"There's nothing you can do," he said. "Everybody's parents die. It's life. Like learning to drive a car."

I used to cry in his car those mornings en route to boarding school. The mornings he told me he was dying of his heart attacks.

He brought me back to the present by saying, "I've led a happy life."

"I know."

However I was surprised at this assessment, not realizing that the reason I was surprised was because I was the one not living a happy life. Was he happy because he had given himself the freedom to be himself? That seemed about all he had done. Maybe that was worth more than I thought.

I hadn't figured out how to do it. Give myself the freedom to be myself. I didn't know that an accomplishment like that takes years to achieve.

But at that moment, sitting there, I decided not to believe him when he said that everyone's parents die. She hadn't died when she said she took the pills and he probably would calcify sitting up at his bar stool.

At the clinic, which masqueraded as a quiet, large family house in Westmount, I lied about the number of abortions. This was my third. I said, first.

I lay down as told to. Once again I gripped the nurse's arm, begging for mercy, begging for kind eyes.

I can withstand this, I told myself.

It's a by-product.

It's just a few hours.

The nurse was gentle with me, more gentle than my mother or father had ever been, and I reveled in those few minutes of being taken care of, even in this awful situation, before the anesthetic took me.

Groggily I finally came awake, unable to fathom what I had done. There was no question in my mind that I was incapable of raising a child. I could barely take care of myself. I myself was still a child. I knew I might always be one.

Afterwards, I sat in a quiet restaurant and ordered a light lunch and told myself here it is, the thing to do is to begin again.

You're purged, cleaned out. It's a kind of power. Begin again.

You're starting all over.

But who was this mother in me that I kept killing?

I didn't think about it exactly in those words but I knew there was a connection. A connection too tangled for me to unravel.

"You look tired," my father said to me at the bar, as I climbed onto a seat next to him. I thought maybe having a drink with him after my little operation might make me sleep.

"Must be anemic," I said.

"Do you want a drink?"

"Alright," I said, even though you weren't supposed to with the anti-biotics they had just given me. But, I had got in the family way by taking chances; I'll stay in the family way with a drink.

"You're unusually quiet," he said.

"Yes."

He didn't ask me what I had done that day.

"How's your health?" I asked, to deflect any conversation about my own. I had slight cramps.

"Terrible."

"What do you mean?"

"Jeanette," he said turning away from me, "Jeanette," he said to the barmaid, "the doctors tell me that I'm past it. That I've got about 3 – 6 months." He wasn't speaking to me.

"Oh Gerald that can't be true," she said from the cash register.

I turned to him. "Really?"

"You can hear, can't you?" What if he isn't making this up? What if he really is going to die? What if he dies and everything's dying and that was when I began crying.

"Daddy you can't really be that sick."

He turned to me, "Well I don't know, don't get that upset. I might live longer."

"You can't. Die, I mean."

"Well why not? Everyone does."

"Maybe they made a mistake. It seems so short," I said wiping my face and pulling at my drink.

"You'll go on. You've got a future," he said.

"I do?" I stared at the bar mirrors.

"Get married and have a child," he said.

"God, there are other things, Daddy."

"Like what?" he asked.

"Like being independent."

"Independent? Is that what you call it? You should be somebody."

"Who?"

"Someone who can be respected."

"How?"

"I don't know. Figure it out for chrissake. You can't rely on me forever."

✳ Twenty-Eight

In my thirties, I stopped drinking. I told my mother, when I visited her in Montreal, that I thought I had drank too much in my life. The problem had been drinking. That's why I could not connect easily. That's why I was shy. I didn't know what it was to not have a drink in my hand.

"Oh," she said. "I just thought you were crazy."

When she replied that way, I could not take the words in. I didn't understand them. Only later did I realize that my incomprehension was a defense against her callousness.

But I was seeing advantages to not drinking. I did not meet men who were like my father. I was forced to talk more if I was out with people. I had to stay with myself.

I thought that was good.

By my forties, I had built a career. I had become an ad writer: clever with words like my mother, working in the movies of consumers' minds.

I never became a creative director or an ad agency vice president. I was more known for being witty, consistent, ambivalent about the business. I always had trouble believing in myself and, thus, I collaborated timidly. I left companies easily, happily even, to move onto the new. I didn't like getting close to people.

Finally I just worked as a lone wolf, thriving as an independent ad writer, servicing companies, never one of them.

In my own hours, I wrote stories that were published, after a long while. The stories took time to be accepted because my world was not the world of most people and, when I wrote stories about my past, editors were not sure. Is this believable? I wrote the stories to make that world of neglect understandable to me. Perhaps if a reader understood it, if they witnessed it also, that would make me comprehend it better myself.

If they understood, it would give such a childhood where no one believed in anything, meaning.

I met a man, the carpenter I told you about, and I married him, even though I never wanted to be married. I thought I was married once in my soul, to my father, and that was enough. The wounded parent always marries the child.

But my lonely poet's son carpenter was persistent with me. By bringing me into the fold, he thought, he would bring himself into the fold too.

I loved being married initially. Someone had committed to me. I could not get over the happiness I felt. My husband was kind and good and I was blessed.

My mother was the last call I made about the wedding. When she finally returned the call, she told me she had been away, visiting a friend in Ottawa. It wasn't that pleasant, she said, the friend is not a very good hostess, and the weather was so very hot. Hotter than New York.

"Yes," I said, "a friend told me that it was very hot up north."

"Must be a weather pattern," she said.

"Listen, I am going to marry Charlie. In a couple of weeks. I have to do something. Go forward in some way. We're not making a big deal of it."

"Oh."

"I'd like you to come, but if you don't want to I understand. It's just a JP thing and a lunch but if you don't want to, don't worry. It's such short notice. I took so long to make up my mind."

I waited a beat.

"You're right," she said gently. "I don't really want to come. It's so tiring you know. Your friends will all be there."

"We'll come to Montreal in the fall," I said ingratiatingly. "We'll do our own celebration."

In a way, I was relieved. I wanted my wedding day to be gay, a party. I wanted it to be about my husband and myself. I did not want the enormous weight of her not liking me.

"Yes that's a much better idea," she said.

"Of course we can take that cruise you want," I said, "in the winter together. Now that I'm married I'll want to get away a lot."

She laughed.

"Well," she said, "I see what you're doing. You're marrying to leave him. I had a thought the other day that you would do that. Plenty of people I know are together for years and then they divorce once they marry. Divorce as friends. Potterton. Howard in England. They marry and then get divorced. It will finalize this endless relationship of yours. I'm not judging it, you and I are very different but you just can't leave anyone. You're not good at leaving like I am," she said. "You'll finally resolve this. You don't want a baby; you would have had one by now. How many years do you have left?"

"About two or three. He has to make money if I am to have a baby. That's our agreement. His making money makes the probability of a baby even less. He can have a baby with his second wife."

"Anyway, I won't come," she said. "It's not like you're some virgin in white having a big wedding."

"No."

Just then the buzzer rang and it was my intended. I motioned that I was talking to her. He sat down.

"Charlie is here. Why don't you say something to him?"

She congratulated him on being so persevering. She told him she couldn't come but so many friends will be there.

I saw his face get smaller. He was not used to being pushed aside. He expected to be celebrated.

He handed the phone back to me, shaking his head.

I told her I would call her when I was on the road, travelling. I was leaving the next morning on business.

She and I discussed how much we like being alone in hotel rooms. How her mother said she used to stare at the wall but, I know didn't I, there was lots going on in her mind.

"I know," I said.

I hung up.

"Are you insulted?" I asked him.

"A little."

"Well, I expected it. And I gave her such little notice. I knew she wouldn't want to come."

"She's so strange," he said.

"True."

But what I didn't say is that I was feeling a kind of love for her. She spoke out my unconscious, that all this is a futile detour from isolation. I just didn't know if it was her voice in me she spoke or the voice of reason.

That night when my husband-to-be and I made love, I didn't turn away like the time before, but I wouldn't let him touch me. I made him stay straight-backed arched, inside me. I held his arms away from me till he came.

I didn't understand it at the time. I didn't understand how hard it was for me to let someone close. There was no name for it in my psyche. Except maybe for blind mother love.

We got married by the sea. Friends had driven long distances, bought gift certificates, dresses and smoked cigarettes in alarm. His family was lending him money and taking planes.

But something was missing.

She had not called nor asked to see pictures nor given a gift.

What it was was that when I stood there in my white dress, among friends who were kind enough to be encouraging, friends who had lived a lifetime with me, some in just long telephone calls, I felt a knife go in. A sharp pierce. Wasn't I supposed to die by now, didn't I know what she knows, love is in the movies, sex is motivation for any killing.

You are so unique; I could hear her saying, in marrying, why not just divorce? Have you no courage?

Oh it was cold, cold glass that I was pushing into my rib cage in my white dress. I was not bleeding red on the white dress, nothing showed, that was my way. I didn't turn her in, she trusted that, she knew I was curious always curious to see what lengths of unlovingness she would get up to next. I turned to her spectre, grabbed my rib and cut my hand as I picked out—like it was nothing—the glass, oh don't bother, it's nothing, an accident. I looked to her missing presence, and thought my life is only an accident. She smiled, anyone's is, how foolish of you to want to play predictably.

Revolution she sneered, bourgeois revolution, are you hurting yet? Sleep with married men in the room not your boring husband you fool. I began listening, some glass still in my rib cage, sinking in, now through my blood vessels, but my heart was safe, I thought, shielded from her, shielded off from her glass, but I found myself leaning toward her while my husband laughed and joked with the guests. I watched her watch me watch her shine her lips in her compact glass mirror. Her eyes shone too. She had me. I was the mirror of darkness, not the heart. What a thing, my husband still talking and there was no need for words while watching her. I was already on the boat with her, watching my own wedding through the prism of her white patent leather shoes, on the boat to see where this place is she is taking me to, that is so free, so artificially sustained, that it so wrongly believes it can live without love.

❊ Twenty-Nine

Five years later, it was my mother who was now lost on the streets of Montreal. When people called her, she didn't answer. Nobody knew where she was. Especially herself.

She asked me, when I went to see her, "How is Charlie?"

"We are divorcing."

"How is Charlie?" she'd ask again.

"We are divorcing," I'd say impatiently. "I wouldn't have a child. I told you many times. He has to have one. I let him go," I said, "so he can meet someone normal and have a baby."

I knew she never paid much attention to what anyone else said, but this behavior seemed a bit more than that.

"How is Charlie?" from her again. She was in her sixties.

Something was wrong.

She was getting muddled in her conversation. And then she would suddenly be fine.

I couldn't tell her that my heart was broken from sabotaging my marriage.

"You lack courage," my husband said. "You turned out fine with lousy mothering. Just try being a mother."

This was fine?

I was frightened to have a child. My mother was inside me and the only way I thought she and I could merge was by my not having a child. Maybe now she'll see me. Maybe now she'll smile at me.

So I chose to be alone, like her. That was where the real women were.

Once he left me, I could not get over the relentless stupidity of it.

Another abortion. This time of my own life.

As I sat visiting with her, after my divorce, I longed for the old fire in her, her quick conversation, and occasionally it shone through, but other times she just sat quietly, and did not know where she had been that afternoon.

"How old are you?" she'd ask, sitting across from me on her couch.

"Forty five," I'd reply.

"How old are you?"

"Maybe you are depressed," I said. "You keep repeating yourself."

"Really?" Here she would snap back into herself.

"Yes, see a doctor."

"Maybe I will."

She stopped driving. And she could not organize any trips for herself, she who had always liked to travel.

"My head," she said, "my head" and she shrugged her shoulders.

I thought maybe it had always been her head. I thought, she never really knew what was going on. She never really listened so maybe this is just an advanced state of narcissism. Maybe this is what happens when your life has always been yourself. It just gets smaller and repetitive and limited.

She asked perfunctory questions and didn't hear the answers. I thought maybe I am just seeing, maybe I am just seeing what always was.

I did not know she, like so many, had Alzheimer's.

But I was beginning to wonder.

✳ Thirty

A few months later my mother stopped using the telephone.

"What happened to Lisbeth?" everyone asked. "There is something wrong."

I called her and, finally when she did answer, she sounded very distant.

I began to wonder what to do and then I received another call. It was Alan, her British boyfriend. Forty years after they met, they were still in constant touch.

"I'm in Montreal," he said, "at your mother's."

"Good, because —"

"My wife just died and I am moving Lisbeth to my house in England. No, I don't think she can come to the phone."

I went to Montreal to help him pack her up. He had already arranged everything. There was nothing for me to do. I sat on her couch and she sat on a chair and just stared.

"Daddy," she said when she looked at him.

To my amazement (and relief), he'd chuckle.

I wondered if he noticed how she never spoke in paragraphs anymore. She just smiled and agreed with everyone. She looked at me once and pointed to her head, and shrugged her shoulders.

They moved to London.

I visited them from time to time. She followed him as a dog does, from room to room. They said they were incredibly happy.

Alan put her on the phone, when I called, and she asked me, politely, as one does on the telephone, even the demented, especially the demented know, to ask, "How are you?" I could not respond because I knew she could not hear.

She kept getting worse.

She could no longer speak. First she lost English. Then she lost German. She went into the hospital with a broken hipbone. He visited her daily, and, when she got out, it was he who taught her how to walk. He managed every aspect of her life, even to changing her diapers. "You realize," he said, as he was driving me to see her in the hospital, "that, as you get old, you become interdependent."

No, I had not realized. I had spent a whole life trying to convince myself of the merits of total independence.

It took him about a year after she arrived in England to admit she was irreversibly ill. "Yes," he said, "you're right. She has Alzheimer's."

"You don't have to stay with her," I said to him. "You can put her in a home."

"No," he said, "I couldn't do that. I am in for the duration."

No matter how much her eyes had glazed to a vacant dullness, he would look at her as if she was still young. "You have no idea how remarkable she is."

She was getting smaller and smaller. I stopped asking to speak to her on the phone. She only responds, he said, to German music. She never looks at anyone.

"She is gone," he said.

✳ Thirty-One

Jeanette and the little man who usually sat behind the gold-plated bars that protected the motel concierge from thieves and drunks, the little man who had sold me many stale cigars throughout my life, for my father, unlocked the door to Room 24 in the Cavalier Motel. I was just seventeen. My father was living in the Cavalier Motel, a rare attempt at practicality.

Jeannette was hugging me. The little man was silent and trying to make himself even smaller.

They opened the door and my father was lying, dead, on the motel bed. The blinds were drawn so the room was as dark as the claws starting to squeeze my heart.

He did not look like himself, now that he had no expression. He looked childlike, quiet. It was just his body that was lying there.

I did not know this familiar looking stranger on the bed. Wrong room.

I stood there, shocked. He was not turning his head toward me to tell me to get a decent life.

I swallowed and tried to breathe. I went up to him and stroked his tie. "I can't stand that North Americans aren't gentlemen," he would say, differentiating himself from them because he insisted on wearing a tie.

His eyes weren't opening.

I took his long fingered hand that did not grab me back and, crying, asked Jeanette and the little man who sold cigars for my father, I asked them to leave.

When they were gone, I put my head down on my father's chest. I lay my head down and cried so it would never end, and he lay there immovable underneath me.

I could not say any words nor think any thoughts. I tried not to cry loudly so people would not hear me. I cried till my chest hurt and then my throat hurt and my chest hurt some more.

He didn't wake up and say, "Stop over dramatizing. This is life and death. It happens to everyone, you fool."

He didn't move.

I sat next to him with my head on him for what seemed like hours. Maybe I would flow into him, help him go wherever he was going, certainly he wasn't meant to go nowhere. I was trying to breathe into him that he be well wherever he was going, when Jeanette knocked on the door and brought me in a dry cc manhattan.

"Drink this," she said.

"Thanks," I said.

"They're 'ere."

"Who?"

"The Montreal hospital people. They take the body."

"What?" I asked terrified.

"They're very nice," she said.

There were two young men standing behind her. They were wearing those nylon black snow jackets that make swishing noises. "We're sorry for your loss," said the one with pimples.

"This is a good thing that he did, leaving his body to science, like this," said the other young man.

Jeanette then told me he had carried a card to that effect. Immediately I knew it was to avoid the cost of a funeral. He was doing me a favor. Another one.

"You should go 'ome," Jeanette said. "Maybe tomorrow you can arrange a service for 'im. Let me know. I will go."

I nodded. I was too tired to wonder which barflies would attend. They seemed to me to be the types who ran away, like bugs, when reality was turned on.

"I guess," I said, exhausted, "I'll go home."

I didn't want to see what those men did.

But I didn't go 'ome. I went to the Boiler Room bar. I was looking for comfort. Lots of cognacs. Maybe that woman who was always sitting there would be there but tonight she wasn't. I thought about going to the woman who had polio but what could she do? She couldn't hold me.

But this was one night I didn't want to be looked at. I didn't want to flirt. I didn't want to have a stupid conversation. I left the Boiler Room.

I began walking. It wasn't a cold night. Spring was coming. I walked from Crescent up Guy to my old school. I thought about ringing the bell and asking for Mother Power.

I cried as I walked. People looked worried when they went by me. Is she all right? I kept walking, gapingly, blindly. But when I got to the convent, I couldn't ring the buzzer.

I wasn't a nun. I wasn't becoming one.

I turned around and walked back down Guy along Sherbrooke past the sturdy buildings that I had so often warmed myself in and on, and turned up Peel to my apartment.

I lay down on my couch.

I grabbed the phone and dialed.

Now it was my voice that was hoarse and rubbernecked.

Mrs. Hill went to get Marilyn.

"Guess what happened now?" I said.

"What?" Her voice was smiling. Like I was going to tell her something funny.

"My father. He died."

"No."

"Yes."

She didn't say anything.

"I can't believe it," I said.

"Are you alone?" she asked.

"Now I really am."

"Can't you call your m-m-m-mother?"

"I don't want to," I said.

"Well- well- well- do you want to come here? I could get some money from my parents to fly you out."

"No. Thanks. I have to take care of things here. He must have a few things to take care of. His clothes. His social security. I should do that."

Jeanette would tell me what to do.

"Maybe he has a little money," I said, "a couple of hundred bucks and I can start somewhere."

Marilyn said nothing. This was different than cerebral palsy. This was soul sickness. This was not her domain. This was mine.

Anyway she was younger than me. I wasn't supposed to need help from her.

She said, "Get some sleep and call me tomorrow. I'll call you—get some sleep first."

"Okay," I said. "Thanks for listening."

But I didn't feel like sleeping. I lay there, feeling like I had been punched. I would call Jeanette for instructions tomorrow. I would go to his apartment and sell his few things. And then, then.

I had to see what she would say. I had to. She must want to know. It's part of her life too. I called that Austrian woman. "Yes?"

"Daddy died."

She was silent a second. "That must be difficult," my mother said coldly.

"It is."

"Well," my mother said, "You two were like a marriage."

So she knew. She knew what it felt like to sit beside him in so many bars. But she was supposed to be the wife and me the daughter.

"You'll get over it," she said. "People do, you know."

I sighed. These two people, my parents. Their mantra was you get over everything. But I wasn't sure.

"He said that too," I said.

"Well he was right."

She was quick to use the past tense.

"How did it happen?"

"He had cancer," I said, "but fortunately he had a heart attack instead."

"He was always waiting for one."

"Yes," I said.

"You should get a job and work your way up. You would be good in advertising or something."

Didn't she know geniuses like myself have to drop out?

"Let me know where you are," she said. "This happens to everyone. You should get a job. Call me in a few days if you like."

That was it. She didn't care. I had no effect on her. She could not love me. How much more proof did I need?

I hung up and began crying. That's it then.

A clean sweep. The orphan picks the fruit off the trees with no hands.

✳ Thirty-Two

Once the bus passed the customs at Rouse's Point in the U.S., I relaxed. I looked out at the one gas station that was affixed to a restaurant in some small border town, the lone houses, the abundance of automotive repair shops.

I had done what I had seen my father do so many times at the border crossing. Lie. "Yes sir I am just visiting the states. I will be back in Montreal in a week."

I had no intention of ever returning.

My plan was to go somewhere sunny and musical with seagulls screeching, somewhere resplendent enough to harbor my dreams. I had just enough money from selling his things to rent a place by the ocean for a few months. Just enough money to get a job and purify myself in the sun, on the sand, by the sea.

I would begin my life as an independent woman.

A woman with straight grey hair and a wrinkle-free face was sitting next to me. She smiled. "Going to see family?" she asked.

"No."

I looked away from her, back out the window.

"Are you from Montreal?"

This while Vermont went lushly by.

"French or English?"

"My father was from England." (I said that as if that fact put order into the world. I wouldn't say or would I that he was from Yugoslavia? From England, as if there might lie some commonwealth for me to tap into.) "He just died."

"Oh I'm sorry."

I looked back out the window. The American trees looked healthier, richer in Vermont. The roads more kempt.

"And now I am starting a new life," I turned back to her.

"Oh really? Are you getting married?"

"Oh no . . ." I said. "I mean a new life, new people."

"Yes?" she asked, a little confused.

She smiled somewhat tenderly. That gave me an idea so I continued, "I mean I want my life to be tender. A new life where people are gentle and caring.

"And sensitive," I continued as if in automatic speaking, "very very sensitive. . . ."

She looked at the back of the bald head in front of her so as not to have to look at me. I didn't care.

I spoke to the bus window and the drum of the road and the farms in the distance, ". . . and no one will try to kill it. I will just be sensitive. And passionate. I will be passionate," I said, trying out words. She turned toward me to see what I would say next.

"This will be my life," I said to the window and the world outside listening, "and then I suppose it will be over. Simple," I turned back to her, "like learning to drive a car."

She looked at me quickly. "Well . . . " she said. She wanted to find a way to place me. "No one at all?"

"No." And as I said it, I felt terribly relieved.

And she did what I expected her to do, and it would take years to change that call and response, she did what I thought I wanted her to do, but I didn't really. What she did was, she turned away.

✳ Thirty-Three

I wish I could tell you that I had been lost in Montreal and then miraculously found, once I crossed the border. That I put myself through college and became a leading psychiatrist for disturbed teenagers and married a maternal loving husband.

Maybe that happens in movies, and even in some lives, but it wasn't what happened to me.

My progress to "normalcy" was record-breakingly slow, and achieved only at the last minute.

I did move to the States and I worked at any job I could get. Eventually I carved a career, just as she had said I would, writing ads, or marketing this and that.

There was my husband and then there were other men, lots of them, for I knew how to attract men. I had learned that, if not much else, at an early age. Mostly they were damaged men. Rebels, iconoclasts. We would instantly recognize each other upon meeting and then go onto spend a lot of time wishing we hadn't.

It didn't take long for even them to figure out I didn't know anything about building a home, being with one person. I was frightened of eating at someone's house; frightened of anything that reeked of domesticity and a world I had not sat at the table at.

It was too painful, for some reason.

In my twenties and maybe even thirties, I thought my inability to conform to a domestic life was interesting. I thought my parents had shaped me to escape the mundane.

I didn't realize they had also shaped me to escape the happiness that comes from the mundane. Safety. Security. Trust. Consistency.

What you build from.

My husband said to me on the second night we were married, "I just figured you out. You don't know how to bond."

It took me ten years to realize he was right. I couldn't. The world was not a loving place to me; try as I tried to make it so. I poured love out to my friends and to lovers at times, but like the proverbial feral cat outside the door, I could not come in. Some feral cats do and I always hoped, hoped I would finally be one of them.

It took me till almost sixty to become tamed. And it was through a form of antibuse. I fell in love—not with a loving man, but with an impossible man who was just like her. A man who couldn't love, witty sometimes, and as resolute not to commit. In his darting eyes, I saw my history replayed and this time, this time I would redeem it. I saw, through how unkindly he treated me and himself, that it was fear that made us not love. He and my mother could not trust after the betrayals they experienced, she with a mother who left her to the Nazis and those she loved being killed, he with parents who had been in the camps.

Both of them became fractured as people and could not recover. Both became Wizards of Oz. My mother and this European man I chose to love were fragile selves propped up behind enormous guilt, shame and coldness. They would not be vulnerable to a world that could be so vile. They refused. And so they refused me.

And this frozenness I perceived as power.

Both times, I tried, in misbegotten ways, to get them to love me. Both times, I failed.

But I opened my heart to him and it hurt, as it had with her. I opened my heart after having closed it as a child.

And this time I survived loving him, even grew from it, so I decided to keep my heart open forever. It just felt better.

A closed heart was more painful than an open one, even an open one that hurt.

Once that was learned, I could begin. Late, yes, yes. Sad, yes, yes. Lost but ultimately found. Like everything else, it just took so long.

I didn't need my defiance anymore.

It turned out I was just another long distance casualty of Hitler, mixed in with some British alcoholism that I embraced and then rejected. A cocktail of confusion and distrust that it took a lifetime to get sober from. It wasn't alcohol I was addicted to. It was pain.

I had to give up sadness and aloneness. Not alcohol.

And so I began a new journey by allowing myself to love.

I was no longer defended against her.

And so I no longer had to run away when I met someone. I was safe, because I could trust in myself.

✳ Thirty-Four

My mother, before Alan came to move her to England with him, would sit in her apartment alone. I thought it was the losing of her looks in her late fifties. I thought she was no longer the star of her movie, and so now she chose to sit alone running reruns. The reality is that it probably was the beginning of her dementia.

Her aloneness got reprieved when Alan's wife died and he came to claim her. A fairy story. Her life ended in a fairy tale.

"I did not kill his wife, you know," she told me.

When I visited her apartment in Montreal while they were getting ready to go, I was hoping she would say goodbye. My adversary was leaving. I was losing the ghost I fought against. What would happen to me now?

I watched her sell her TV, her bed. She was shipping her furniture and artwork. I furtively took two records that I had listened to as a young girl in her apartment. I was hurt that she did not offer me anything, but that was an old story.

Before she completely lost her mind, I would telephone her in London. That's when she still had fragments of a mind. She would say she was just thinking about me. "Isn't that odd?" she'd ask.

Her boyfriend raised seven children so now he raised her. He lost all his money in Lloyd's so they lived off her money.

I visited them in London but only for tiny periods.

I had been married and divorced and she could not grasp it. I would fall in love and she could no longer ask what he was like in bed. Neither of us could look strangely at each other anymore when I told her I could not stay with anyone. I did not need to hide from her the knowledge that I always felt she was lurking inside any man I love.

With her mind gone, she did strange things. She shuffled around Alan's huge house saying, "Jacqueline bought us theatre tickets and she is angry at us that we did not go."

"What does she mean?" Alan asked me.

She means, I thought, we missed our cue.

She said, "I quite like you, you know. I wish you'd known me before."

She was sitting in one of Alan's huge chairs.

She was right. I wish I had known her before. Before the war. Before so much fear had taken over her psyche that her only defense was to hurt.

When she was well, she believed I should be grateful for what she gave me.

And she was right. She gave me life. And she gave me a broken indomitableness.

"I made you strong," she told me, when she had not yet lost her mind.

"I really did," she would say to people. "I made her strong. Jacqueline is a survivor. She's just like me," she said. "Everyone says so."

Community

Join the community of readers discussing *Lost in Montreal*.
Scan the QR code below with your smartphone.

About the Author

Gay Walley is the author of two prior novels. *Strings Attached* (University Press of Mississippi, 1999) was a finalist for the Pirates Alley/Faulkner Award, the Writer's Voice Capricorn Award, and Paris Book Festival Award.
She is also a Zoetrope finalist for her story, "The Naked Maja".
Her play *Love, Genius and a Walk* opened at the 2013 Midtown Festival in New York and was nominated for six awards including best playwright. It is scheduled to be produced Off-Broadway.
Gay Walley lives in New York City.